MY DEVOTION

Julia Kerninon

MY DEVOTION

*Translated from the French
by Alison Anderson*

Europa
editions

Europa Editions
214 West 29th Street
New York, N.Y. 10001
www.europaeditions.com
info@europaeditions.com

Copyright © Rouergue, 2018
First publication 2020 by Europa Editions

Translation by Alison Anderson
Original title: *Ma dévotion*
Translation copyright © 2020 by Europa Editions

Library of Congress Cataloging in Publication Data is available
ISBN 978-1-60945-614-6

Kerninon, Julia
My Devotion

Book design by Emanuele Ragnisco
www.mekkanografici.com

Cover image: Pixabay

Prepress by Grafica Punto Print – Rome

Printed and bound in Great Britain by Clays Ltd, Elcograf S.p.A.

CONTENTS

For A., once again,
who arranged things so that I could finish
this book in the weeks and months
that followed the birth of our baby.

And now at last
I got a good look at you
—TED HUGHES, *Birthday Letters*

MY DEVOTION

LONDON

When I was twenty-five, I wrote a slim essay devoted to Hans Christian Andersen. I was young at the time, and thought I'd offered convincing proof of the close ties between the Danish author's life and work, but I was kidding myself. Years later, when I actually read it—in other words, read it like a book someone else might have written, which is what it had indeed become—I was stunned by what I found. Instead of the pertinent analyses I seemed to recall, I encountered page after page of an almost lyrical defense of isolation, and I heard the muted voice of the young woman I had been—an introverted girl, hiding behind her books, as terrified as she was proud, and fiercely attempting to impose order upon the world. Evoking in succession the poverty that had marked Andersen's youth, his inexplicably poor reputation in his native country, the spare language of his fairytales, and his talent for paper-cuts, I was unwittingly telling a tale of resistance, of an entire life lived in spite of others, and magnified through fiction. But there was something else in my text that I'd completely forgotten about: I devoted a great deal of space (a disproportionate amount, in fact, since the topic took up forty pages out of a hundred) to the falling-out between Andersen and Charles Dickens. The two writers had met in the month of June, 1847, during a visit Andersen made to London with a view to halting piracy of his works in England. He was just beginning to be known outside Denmark, and when he met Dickens in a London drawing room, it seemed he instantly fell in love, and while his love may have remained Platonic, the force of it was still devastating. His letters are overflowing with childish testimonies to his love, but Charles Dickens had a very different personality. When the English novelist wrote back and perfunctorily extended his hospitality, he'd clearly never imagined that Andersen would take him at his word. In March, 1857, however, a delighted Andersen showed up at Dickens's family home in Kent. He stayed for five weeks—sufficient time for the entire family, including the children, to end up detesting him. After his departure, Andersen never heard from his friend again. This was the real story nesting inside the first book I wrote: a severed friendship, an unrequited love. I wrote the book in 1963, in Amsterdam, in the house where I'd been living with you for seven years, and where we would live for another decade or more before parting a first time, then getting back together and going off to share another house together for fourteen years until our brutal separation. When I left my house just now I had no idea I would run into you on this pavement in Primrose Hill, coming straight towards me as if by magic, holding a crumpled brown paper bag in your hand which, you would inform me after a moment, contained two little cinnamon rolls. No doubt you would like to ask me how I am and give me your news, but I have been thinking about you for twenty-three years, every day of your absence, so this time you won't be doing the talking, Frank. I will, and I alone. I'm going to tell you everything, here and now, standing in the street, I'm going to tell you our entire story right from the start, because I have to hear it, too. I can't stop looking at you—Frank, lost and then found. Let me begin.

D espite my surprise at finding you here in London, of all places, walking straight at me down Adelaide Road, I recognized you at once. And yet, after I called out to you and hugged you, once I began really looking at you, I wondered how I could have known so instinctively that it was you beneath that weathered face of an old man. While you were talking, smiling your impossible smile, I somehow managed to work out that in the autumn you would turn eighty. I could scarcely believe it. It only took a few seconds for my eyes to grow accustomed to your new appearance, to overcome it even, like a horse facing a jump, and I managed to see you, *you*, beyond the wrinkles and the white hair. You hadn't changed a bit; in fact, you were almost painfully familiar. Frank Appledore. For twenty-three years I have never stopped hoping I would see you again before we die—how could I have known that we lived only a few streets from one another? There you stand before me, in the cool April air, you are wearing a bulky woolen coat that makes you look like a colonel, your face is tanned, and I can still see the scar on your ear lobe from the hole you pierced in it years ago. As you talk, Frank, I can see your teeth, and it looks as if you fixed the right canine you broke in an accident, which year was that, a year I wasn't around. I remember that's what you used to say, *I don't have accidents when you're around, Helen, with you I'm safe*, you said, often, as if regretfully. In your eyes my finest quality, caution, was worthless. And yet that was why your father had agreed to entrust you to me, even though you were a few months older than I was. Remember? When we went to live in Amsterdam, I was the one, I alone, who pleaded our cause with our parents, because I had that authority. I didn't always keep you safe, but I tried my best. I promise you. It's you, you haven't changed, at the age of eighty you still look like the young man I knew—but you are also like the home town one returns to only to find that in one's absence a favorite building has been destroyed and replaced by a Starbucks. You're an old man, now, Frank. With me around, you didn't have accidents. There was always my caution, and forever your scorn. If I hadn't spent more than half of your life with you, you'd be dead by now, and that's a fact. No man, Frank, is a hero in the eyes of the woman who knows him best.

P eople swore I'd lose my memory as I got older, but they were wrong, just as when I was seventeen they swore that one day I would find out that real life was not to be found in books. That was wrong, too. I haven't given up all hope of understanding the lies adults tell before I die. Now, as before, my attention span is slightly superior to the norm. The fact that all through my early years I was constantly on the lookout—as a child, to make sure my brothers wouldn't kill me; as an adolescent, in hopes of eluding their shared goal of raping me—left me extremely alert to everything going on around me. Because my father, like yours, was a diplomat, I learned very early on to detect the insinuations of adult discourse, and later, when I myself was an adult—at least as far as the rest of the world was concerned—I was never able to abandon my watchfulness. A child of embassies, I grew up in a world where the most important thing was to know the codes and respect them, to understand what someone wanted before he himself knew. In case you're wondering, I've been living in London for eight years. You see? I finally returned to my father's country, I've finally become what I had thought I never could be, deep down—an Englishwoman. Moving house at the age of seventy-two is a fairly strange experience, but my solitude has at least relieved me of other people's concern. No one worries about me, apart from a handful of individuals who are also old enough not to be able to claim to protect me, so in the end all I had to do was contact a moving company who transported my furniture to my destination without asking any questions. I found a three-room flat not far from the British Library, and since then I have spent my days reading, as I have done all my life. At times I am still surprised to find myself here. I look out the window and think, *London? But why London?* And I immediately remember. After what happened to us in Normandy, I initially returned to live on my own in Amsterdam. Because I was in a daze—I can find no other explanation for it now. I simply went back to the place where I had a house—a house where I'd lived with you for so long that, in fact, it was the worst possible place to hope to seek refuge. And yet, inexplicably, I held on for a number of years, and went on living there. But when the city finally decided to put a plaque in your honor on the front of the building, I packed my bags as quickly as possible, trying very hard not to cry, and in spite of everything a part of me—why hide it now— was terribly proud to think that it had come to this. Have you ever been there, have you seen the plaque? A square of heavy pinkish copper: *In dit gebouw begon de schilder Frank Appledore zijn carrière*—it unsettles me as much for what it doesn't say as for what it does.

Were there ever two people more different than you and I? You respected nothing; I respected everything. You had a talent for joy, as intensely as I had a talent for labor. You were glowing, indifferent, incapable of doing anything that didn't interest you; I took a sort of immoderate pride in my ability to submit, to wear my eyes out reading line upon line of tiny characters, and always, always, my ability to anticipate the expectations of others. I was attentive, the way an animal is attentive. I perceived sounds and smells that eluded others, my hypersensitivity made me both very empathetic and utterly tyrannical: since I knew everything, I wanted to take charge of everything. Later, my husband would ask, amused, back in the days when I could still amuse him: *But why did you go into publishing, Helen, when you have the soul of a captain?* The answer is simple, and always has been: *Because when you were an ambassador's daughter, born in the late 1930s, a captain wasn't something you became.* My husband should have known this, but I think that like most men in those days, he actually knew very little of substance when it came to the lives of the women he frequented, including his own wife. You, too, Frank, belonged to that era. I think you are a good person—deep down probably much better than I am—but you see only what interests you. You disregard all the rest. And that is surely the reason why in my tiny little domain I'm a specialist, and you are an artist. Like the canvases you paint, their images forming layer by layer, until all at once they become perfectly visible, what happened to us took years in the making. But I think that our temperaments, right from the start, already contained the seed that would cause our ruin and the death of an innocent person.

The year of my birth Prime Minister Neville Chamberlain, terrified by the possibility of a second world war, went on a diplomatic mission to Munich to meet Hitler, which he concluded by giving his consent to the German occupation of Czechoslovakia. My father was part of the delegation. Chamberlain was sixty-nine years old at the time, and had only two years left to live. My father was about to turn forty, an ideal age for a diplomat. He had joined the Foreign Office at the end of the Great War. I think what he had done, exactly, during that conflict, can be summed up in one word: lying. I do not know what role he played in Bad Godesberg during those few days in September, 1938. (You didn't ask your father that sort of question, back then. You handed him the sugar tongs once a day, at tea time, and that was about it.) What I do know is that it was undoubtedly due to this questionable loyalty that my father was sent to safety in Switzerland for the duration of the war, and went on to become minister of the embassy in Bern, on Thunstrasse. Then, in the confusion of the post-war years, when all of Europe was still reeling from the clash of nations, he was posted to Trieste and Athens, and finally, in 1950, appointed ambassador to the embassy of the United Kingdom in Rome. Before all this, when he was thirty-three, he had been in Amsterdam on business, where he met my mother at a dinner party hosted by her elder brother in May, 1931, married her two months later, and then conceived Fred, Maarten, and me, in the space of seven years. I was the youngest. My father was a bad father, but a good orator—a hard man, but eloquent, and every year, his Saint George's Day speech brought tears to the eyes of the British expatriates gathered in the gardens of the Villa Wolkonsky in Rome. Do you remember? I was the only daughter of that man, but I've never been able to *speak*. I have written tens of thousands of words in my life, but to speak them aloud has always seemed painfully beyond reach. If only I'd spoken to you in time, Frank. If only, just once, I'd said something instead of simply *doing*, always doing, always doing everything, if only I'd known how to use those words which, in their written form, were my consummate skill; if I had known how to tame them so that they would carry my voice, none of this would have happened, would it? That is why I am speaking now, and you must listen.

Rome

Our story begins at the Villa Wolkonsky, where Nikolai Gogol wrote *Dead Souls*, and which, when we were living there, housed the embassy of Great Britain in Rome. My father was the ambassador. Your father was Deputy Head of Mission. In the photograph that glows in my memory like a candle, we are all there. My father, John Gabriel, a full martini in his hand, staring at the camera lens without the slightest intention of smiling. Next to him, my mother, her hair a bright halo, her nose slightly wrinkled because of the light. Your father, Horatio, laughing, arms spread, leaning against a decorative palm tree, while your mother, Kate, sitting at least three feet away from him, directs her dreamy gaze at the viewer. Your brother Adrian is standing behind her, looking at the floor. The group portrait is of no interest to him. My two elder brothers are in the background talking, their hands, caught in motion, are blurred. They are extraordinarily handsome, but when I look at this part of the image, it seems to glow red with something evil. I am a bit farther off, arms crossed, knees squeezed tight, looking straight ahead. And you are right next to me, imitating my position, and smiling with your mouth wide open. It's summer in Rome. There we are. Nowadays you're a famous painter, maybe even that *dying* painter, if what I have read in the papers recently is true, but when I met you, you were only twelve years old, like me. And of course, you weren't painting back then—in fact, you didn't paint at all until you were twenty-eight years old, contrary to the legends your admirers have been chattering about—but perhaps I'm the last person alive to know this now, and when I suddenly realize it, I shiver at the thought that the world we knew, the world into which we were born and where we grew up, that world no longer exists, has vanished altogether. Our parents died, one after the other. Adrian is dead. My brothers, too, eventually died—Fred first, in a hunting accident, fifteen years ago, and Maarten a year or two later, from pancreatic cancer. Let them burn in hell—slowly. Only you and I are left now, the eternal youngest children, the only survivors of the many group portraits we took back then. National holidays, New Year's, the Queen's birthday, Remembrance Day—in my mind, relentlessly, I zoom in on these images, one after the other, I swoop like a raptor onto those two blurry faces among all the others, trying to recall that distant time when we were younger than everyone at the British embassy in Rome, where your father and mine governed hand in hand, and where our mothers languished, each in her own way, hating each other with such intensity that only a well-dosed martini could make them laugh together, an identical, strangled laugh, heads thrown back as if burdened by their lacquered chignons—our idle, sublime mothers, whom I swore never to resemble.

It all began in the autumn of 1950. Your family had arrived in Rome one week before mine, and a dinner was organized at your place to establish contact after we moved in. Our fathers had already met on numerous occasions, naturally, although the exact circumstances of their encounters had never been explained to us, but I knew from experience that the introduction of the two families who were preparing to run the embassy together was part of an inevitable ritual protocol. In every city our fathers' ambition had taken us to, we children performed our duties as well, after a fashion. While we were moving in I had already noticed you in the corridors of the villa, drifting wordlessly by like a shadow, or watching me through a window like some character in an unnerving Brontë novel, but I ignored you the way you ignored me, preserving my strength for the coming battle: that first endless, obligatory dinner which we knew we would soon have to endure. A few days after our arrival, with all our cases finally unpacked, we went to ring one evening at the massive door to your apartment—my parents, my two brothers, and I. When your mother opened it, I saw you both behind her, you and Adrian, wearing your dress shirts and trousers, leaning against the fireplace and radiant with ill will. Our mothers—and it is hard for me to believe that they did not both know, from the first gaze, how much they would despise each other for the entire length of their cohabitation—exchanged the customary effusive pleasantries before shoving us towards each other and babbling our names and ages in passing. Adrian was already nineteen that year and had only gone with his parents to Rome because he wanted to pursue his Latin studies there, and he soon slunk off somewhere. My brothers, who were seventeen and eighteen, who had been two deplorably mindless children and were about to become two deplorably mindless men, were brutally violent adolescents in those days, utterly thick, and I realized at the very start that you had grasped this perfectly. The adults had wandered into an adjacent living room in a cloud of words, while my brothers were sniffing around like dogs, in search of an ashtray and a bottle of strong alcohol, which meant that you and I suddenly found ourselves quite alone together. And that was when you said these words, shrugging one shoulder towards the double doors that led into your dining room:

"Do you hate your family, too?"

Oh, Frank. I remember those words as if they were the first sensible thing I'd ever heard in my entire life.

When you asked me that extraordinary question—*Do you hate your family, too?*—in an instant I felt closer to you than to anyone I had ever known. It was, perhaps, the dominant feeling I experienced at that time: a hatred of my family, equal only to my love of books. Do you remember what people used to say at embassy receptions, all those years we lived together in Rome? As we huddled beneath the table, we could hear how they lavished pity on my poor mother for having me as a daughter. *Maaike is perfectly gorgeous, such a shame her daughter can't hold a candle to her, though she is charming, of course.* To my face they always said I was charming, but never that I was pretty—and when I think back to all those absurd lies we used to hear at the villa, I am *hurt* by the very thought that no one, ever, thought of lying to me, simply to make me feel more at home in my own skin. There is a scene in *Tess of the d'Urbervilles* where Tess has just moved into the d'Urberville home with her young husband, Angel, and together they come upon ancestral portraits hanging on the wall of two women who resemble Tess—but hideously: *her fine features were unquestionably traceable in these exaggerated forms*, writes Hardy, mercilessly. I believe this must be more or less what my mother saw when she looked at me, because my face was an ordinary version of her own—like in the novel, where the portraits are built into the masonry, so that the lovely Tess, despite her humiliation, cannot remove them. And yet I wasn't that ugly—I had simply failed to meet the goal that had been set before my birth, to serve as heir to my mother's beauty, to carry her reputation as a beautiful woman far and wide. My name, Helen, that of a woman so ravishing she started the very first war in Western literature: I wore it like a tiara that was far too heavy for me. However, while I could not help being hurt, I was not vain enough to indulge the fantasies of the adults who were raising me, and I quickly accepted my fate and my full, sturdy, small body—I never grew taller than the height I had reached by the age of thirteen, five foot one; my features were mundane, with no delicacy: greenish-gray eyes, black hair, and a tiny, pointed face, with tight lips and a sharp nose. I wore my hair short, just below my ears, to emphasize my eyes, which were of no use to me except for reading. I could read in four different languages, and I read everything. My mother silently held this against me, as if she thought that I hadn't made an effort when I was still in her womb, and that her beauty had passed me by, like some ball I'd been too clumsy to catch. *Poor Maaike*, went the refrain, not three feet away from me, the tone quite pleased. As I hid under the table with you I wept buckets onto your shoulder. We did not know, Frank, that much later you would paint me to console me for that insult. You would paint me surrounded by my attributes, just as I was, with my books and pens, my worried gaze, my simple clothes, in my study, my bath, my bed, in taxis, shaded parks, wherever I went. My very ordinary figure would be displayed on your huge canvases, and I believe that, in oil, no one could find fault with me. I would become eternal, in my way. And no one, no one at all would ever remember my mother.

y father, undoubtedly, will be remembered by the men he offended, and they are legion. Your father would become the most famous—famous in the little world in which we lived—so badly did my father treat him during the six years that followed. *The cohabitation between Merton and Appledore must have been one of the most poignant in history,* I read recently, in the memoirs of the former office secretary. (And I had to read those words several times over, I confess, before I understood that he was not referring to you and me.) Throughout their time in Rome my father employed every form of humiliation he'd learned over his long career against yours, and in the end your father humiliated him in return, using the only method my father knew nothing about. But I digress. To get back to that first dinner: gathered around the table were our fathers—determined to tear each other apart, loving our mothers badly, and totally absent in our upbringing—and then our mothers—disillusioned and selfish, their mutual hatred already like a lamp casting a harsh light over the table. There was Adrian, your very serious older brother, who would become a minister at about the age of thirty, after he had married a young woman from the same village as your father. Later, he obtained the high rank of ecclesiastical inspector, which he occupied with perfect integrity for seven years. When I went to see him in 1978, taking advantage of a trip I made to England not long after his appointment, he greeted my customary congratulations with an apologetic smile. *I'm a cleric in my father's village, and Frank is traveling all around the world with his painting. Why ever should you congratulate me, Helen? I was the eldest. I was respectful, the way the eldest nearly always is. I didn't know it was possible. Do you understand? I didn't know it was possible to say no.* There was a passion in his voice I had never heard before. He died two months later, surrounded by his wife and five children. The last thing he said to me that day, after walking me to the little gate at the edge of his garden, still echoes in my mind. *The truth shouldn't be able to hurt us, Helen.* And I still see the magnificent room where the dinner was held, that first evening, in Rome. Filled with emotion, I thought, Gogol was in this room, and Sir Walter Scott, and Stendhal. I looked all around me, but my gaze avoided my brothers' faces, across from me. Back then I had no words to describe what my brothers did to me. Later, once I knew the words, I almost felt sorry. Later that evening, at the dinner table, during dessert, you leaned towards me slightly on your chair and in a hushed voice you said:

"But what are we going to do? How are we going to get out of this?"

And so, I believe, from that very first evening, there was one thing I knew for certain, Frank: it would be my fate to watch over you.

I t all went so quickly, in the beginning—as if the celluloid of my memory had been overexposed in those early years, and it was impossible for me to recall the precise order of words and gestures, offerings, contributions, rewards, arms around shoulders, mutual gratitude, and shared language, which brought us closer, you and I, and created a bond, forever. *Whatever happens*, writes Rainer Maria Rilke in one of his Requiems, *has had such a head start on our suppositions that we can never catch up with it, never experience what it really looked like.* In the autumn of 1950 I started going to school with you every morning, the Marymount International School. The chauffeur who came for us would stop outside the door, and you were always a bit late, you would climb in next to me on the rear seat, and we would talk and talk. We were united in our sidereal hatred of our parents and their witty remarks, their despicable activities, and their heartlessness. In the spring of 1953, your father and my mother became lovers. After three years of putting up with my father's affronts, Horatio got his revenge by seducing the ambassador's stunning wife. Oh, but my mother wasn't innocent, either. I think she had been waiting for nothing else, ever since that first dinner party—to take revenge on my father for his lack of interest in her and to hurt your mother. And yet for the two of us this disturbance held nothing but advantages: out of their depth, our parents paid us no attention, and we could spend our nights wandering through the sleeping city and talking, talking endlessly. A year later, once everyone knew about this most poorly hidden secret of international diplomacy, your mother upped and left your father and moved into a château somewhere outside Paimpol. Imperturbable and secretive, she had acquired it unbeknownst to her husband or sons as she meticulously planned the destination of her imminent flight. She would live there until her death, in that magnificent dwelling surrounded by an estate that was literally brimming with horses, alone with her servants and her animals. You never forgave her. As for me, with every passing day I have come to understand her better and better.

The year Kate left, I was sixteen. My brothers, too, were
growing up. I would run into them in the corridors of
the house with their trousers down, touching their
privates, they would shoot burning gazes at me, and hide
handkerchiefs soiled with semen under my pillow or even
between the pages of my books. It was disgusting, humiliating,
abnormal; my underpants disappeared inexplicably one after
the other, my mother turned a blind eye. The only time I'd tried
to broach the subject with her—deeply shocked at the time, at
the age of ten, to have this major danger looming over me—she
swatted away my fear with the back of her hand, the way she
would swat at a cloud of smoke from her cigarette. She seemed
almost proud, to be honest, of her sons' virility, she was like
some medieval chatelaine puffed up about the rapes and mas-
sacres committed by her offspring, their ability to ravage the
surrounding countryside. To flatter her pride, they had both
signed up for a class on Greco-Roman wrestling, and I would
see them come home still gleaming with oil and lasciviously
unwinding the protective straps from their hands, never taking
their eyes off me. They terrorized me. You were the only one I
could talk to. When I think about Rome, that's what I remember—being small, anxious, misunderstood, spending a colossal
amount of energy protecting myself from my brothers, liking
only books and you. In fact, I loved you then, Frank, more
than anything. You were my reason for living. And one evening
in 1954 I would not leave your room. I didn't say, *let's do it*, I

didn't say, *take me*, but you knew why I was there, and I recall your elated expression as you came inside me. Later, as we lay side by side in the silence of the sleeping villa, you whispered:

"Shouldn't we have put a towel down, or something?"

"What for?" I asked.

"For the blood. Girls bleed the first time, don't they?"

"Yes," I whispered, not moving.

"You see. So there must be blood on the sheets. We'll have to find a way to hide them. Wait, let me look."

You switched on the little lamp above your bed, and very gently pulled away the sheets around me to take a careful look. You didn't know much about girls in those days, but you knew you had to withdraw before it was too late, and that, the first time, they would bleed. This was the 1950s, after all. In Italy, the Fascist laws against contraception were still in effect. When *La Dolce Vita* came out, marking the beginning of a new era, we had already left the city behind four years earlier. Fellini's Rome, the Rome of American movie stars on the via Veneto, of plunging necklines and propitious fountains: we missed all that. Our Rome was the Rome of Pope Pius XII and his god-awful speeches, of censure, of post-war poverty.

"There's no blood," you said eventually, puzzled.

I didn't move. I held my breath. You were trying to figure it out.

"Do you think perhaps I didn't do it properly?"

"No, you did it very well, Frank."

"But then there should be blood, shouldn't there? The first time . . ."

That was when you understood. You stopped suddenly and looked at me, and I burst into tears.

"Helen, Helen, Helen," you muttered, rocking me in your arms. "Helen, Helen, Helen."

That night, as if to erase what my brothers had done to me,

we made love again in the pitch black Roman night, silently, clenching our teeth to keep from waking anyone, and we did it once again in the early morning, as if we were needlessly retracing our steps to make sure we'd locked the door properly behind us.

Something else happened that year. While trying to figure out how to get away from my family, one day, I suddenly remembered the apartment my mother owned in Amsterdam. When she was still an adolescent both her parents died of an illness a few months apart, and since her eldest brother at the time was twenty-four years old and was already working for the family firm, he had immediately taken charge of the business. Thus, nothing changed for my mother; she went on living in the family home, without her parents, with her five brothers and sisters. When she received her inheritance at the age of twenty-one, she bought herself the three-story apartment on the Prinsenstraat where she lived until she married my father, two years later, in June 1930. I had never set foot in the place, I'd only heard her mention it. I knew it existed, in other words, that somewhere far away there was a place that belonged to the family inheritance, a place my brothers would never dream of living in, and which I could therefore lay claim to for our sole benefit: for you and me. The first time I spoke to my mother about my idea, she looked at me warily:

"What exactly do you want to go and do in Amsterdam?"

"Study."

"Study what?"

"Literature."

"Dutch literature?" she asked, raising an eyebrow ironically.

"All literature, Mother," I replied, unable to hold back a shiver of pleasure as I did so. *Leave this house. Read books. Read in peace. Never come back.* It was as if I could hear the words pounding in my temples.

"And what makes you think you can do that in Amsterdam?"

"There's a university there, and I will read books."

"*Boeken,*" sighed my mother in Dutch, turning her splendid profile towards the window. "*Boeken.* Books. Always books, Helen. I left Amsterdam, I left my country for your father, I wanted to see the world, and so I took you with me, you, my children, all over Europe, and now you, my daughter, Helen, you want to go back to Amsterdam to read books. You live in Rome, in eternal sunshine, and you want rainy Holland. Why?"

She seemed sincerely curious, but I was thinking that the easiest answer to her question would be:

Because if I stay here, my brothers will go on raping me.

There was no point in saying it, in giving this answer, because my mother would not hear it. So I said, "I simply thought that maybe I could go and live in your old apartment."

"*My* apartment?"

"Yes. With Frank."

She seemed to be considering my request, clearly surprised that her lackluster youngest child could come up with such an idea. And yet—something I have known now for a long time— if I hadn't ventured into the breach back then, without knowing exactly where I was headed, if I hadn't stood up to my parents to get them to let me move to Amsterdam in the autumn of 1956, not only would I not have had this life, but surely, rather, I would not have had any life at all. Paradoxically, I was extremely lucky, precisely because they underestimated me. It was because I was of no interest to my parents that they let me go, that they really did not care where I went to get away from them. This indifference, and our milieu full of diplomats, and the fact that you were supposed to be my chaperon—against all expectation, it was enough to sway them. When I spoke to you about my project, I assumed you would think it over before you committed—because that's what I would have done, naturally—but you simply wanted me to describe the city to you before we went there. And so, time after time during our nocturnal rambles, I told you about Amsterdam's misty streets, which I had never seen, but I'd read descriptions in books—the placid canals, the tall houses with their narrow staircases, the flower market. I had no plans for you, but at least I had found us a place, a destination. All you had to do— all *we* had to do—was pass our final exams.

The day of the exam results, after we'd found my name on the list of those who'd passed, we searched for your name in vain. You had failed. With me you have always insisted that, paradoxically, it was a good sign, as if missing that step was not a humiliation but indeed an honor, a mark of intelligence and of an exceptional nature, but the fact that you never spoke about it to anyone, that you never even tried, later on, to include this event in your artist's legend—which would have been easy enough, and it would surely have worked to your advantage—this convinced me all the more firmly that deep down you were disappointed. In fact, it is possible to see this defeat as the beginning of the difficult decade that lay ahead of you, and which would only really come to an end when you began to paint. Nowadays your name might instantly evoke success, but the first ten years of your adult life were nothing but a painful series of failures. The day we got the results, however, we did not know that, so we walked ever so slowly back to the Villa Wolkonsky, trying to work out how we would break the news to our parents, and how to convince them to let us leave together for Amsterdam just as we'd been planning for months now. We both thought the prospect of you repeating your year was unacceptable, because it meant we would be apart. I would remain at the mercy of my brothers, while you would be moping around the consulate in Milan, where your father was about to be transferred. You claimed to be hopping mad, but I knew that deep down you were desperate at the thought that you'd disappointed me, that you'd failed to protect me the way you had sworn you would, and you kicked at the tree trunks as we walked along. You simply couldn't imagine that you might be able to convince your parents to let you leave after all.

"They'll never agree," you said over and over, sadly.

"No, they won't agree," I said eventually. "But they'll *accept* it. That's different."

I was preoccupied by thoughts of the coming altercation, but also embarrassed to be walking beside you with my diploma virtually an accomplished fact while you had nothing. We had not envisioned this possibility, even when I was scrupulously reviewing my notes while you pretended to be reading, lying on a sofa next to me, as if simply combining our efforts in everything meant it would suffice for only one of us to study in order to pass our exams. I had always been the conscientious one, timid and respectful of the established order, and although my marks may have been higher than yours all through secondary school, I had respectfully seen you as someone who viewed studying as inconsequential, since thus far you'd managed to make it through each consecutive school year without difficulty. Why your method had not worked this time, I don't know. But there was something rather terrifying about this fiasco, because for the first time I could see the limits of your system, and I think you could, too. When you suggested we run away, it initially indicated a desire to stay hidden, the way certain animals do when they know they are about to die. You were wounded in your self-esteem, to have been brought low by school, an institution for which you had so little respect. It is always nobler to scorn only that which you are able to sail through gracefully; to belittle the authority that has deemed you unworthy shows a failure of magnanimity. So we walked along, gloomy and worried on that luminous day in May, and my unease grew ever greater until eventually it became a solid thing. I could feel determination rising in me, the likes of which I had never known, and I believe that it was from the force of my anger and astonishment that I drew the strength, that very evening, to confront our principal adversary, your father—as if I was seeking, by obtaining the right for you to come with me to Amsterdam after all, to erase your failure, to deny it and restore the balance between us. In a way that was how I won the battle, which for us was decisive— because the best way to subdue an enemy is to speak his own language. I was the daughter of the ambassador, you were the son of the Deputy Head of Mission—our academic imbalance cruelly rekindled the imbalance that had divided our fathers over the last six years—and this would work to our advantage. The fact you'd failed to obtain your diploma might at first have seemed a private, family matter—but in the little world of the embassy it was no such thing, *a fortiori* when the child of a rival passed with flying colors. I realized this the moment I started talking to Horatio—in fact, he was my greatest ally in the matter, because he was the only person who desired as greatly as I did to forget—or rather, in his case, to *make others forget*— your failure at school. When I told him the results he murmured:

"The little cretin. The little son of a bitch."

I t took him a moment to remember my presence. He lit a
cigarette to regain his composure, and forcing a smile out
of his dull diplomat's mouth he said:
"And you? How did you get on, Helen?"
"It went very well," I said.
"*Very* well? Good marks, all As?"
"Yes," I said, because it was true. "All As."
And on seeing his expression I knew I would win. I laid out
my arguments, one after the other, but I didn't even have to use
all of them. All Horatio wanted at that point was a solution,
and I had one ready-made for him. You would come and live
with me in the apartment in Amsterdam where, as my parents
had already agreed some time ago, I would begin my studies in
literature. You would enroll in a correspondence course and
prepare to re-sit the exams the following spring in the utmost
discretion. We would be together; we would be studious and
reasonable. You had just left school. You didn't need to go to
class. You simply needed a second chance, and I was convinced that under these circumstances you'd be ready to seize
it, because, in a way, I would lead by example. I could even
help you study. I don't think Horatio ever really cared much
for me—not only was I the daughter of his worst enemy, but
our temperaments were too antagonistic, my restraint annoyed
him, offended something within him, this man who was so san-
guine and intuitive, and in his way, he was afraid, I believe, of
what I might think of his affair with my mother. He feared my

opinion, and yet I believe he also respected me for never saying anything to anyone. In his way, he valued me for being so
different from him, although neither one of us had anything to
do with that. On occasion I had despised him, but I had always
recognized his good qualities. He was not a fool. He was a man
of highly questionable morals, but he was certainly not devoid
of intelligence or finesse. On the contrary, he was clever, sharp,
even funny at times, and he knew when something was in his
best interest. He let us go.

S ummer 1956 was spent visiting our respective families in England—you in Bedfordshire and I in Dorset, so we only met up again in August, outside the door of the apartment, each of us coming from a different place and yet inexplicably punctual—and I recall the emotion I felt on seeing you coming round the corner of the street with your cases, while I'd been walking down that street for only a few minutes, and how, never taking our eyes off each other, step by step, we ended up facing one another outside the right address—like today. I never tire of looking at you, I cannot believe you are here before me, I have so many things to tell you, I cast my mind back through the years and my memory is endless, ruthless. I cannot interrupt or even slow the movement of reminiscence. That summer, the summer we left, something else happened, miles away from Amsterdam on the far side of the Atlantic Ocean, and neither you nor I knew anything about it. In a hamlet in New York State, the receptionist in a beauty salon found herself invited by a client to spend the weekend with her on Long Island in her lover's house. So they took the morning train together, and the lover came to fetch them at the station in his car and drove them to his place. Later the three of them set off in his Oldsmobile for a concert. The lover was angry, because he didn't want to go to the concert—it was his companion who had insisted—and to show his defiance he'd got drunk. On a bend on an isolated road he lost control of the vehicle, and it careened into the woods at over seventy miles an hour—according to his mistress's subsequent testimony in a controversial book. The lover and the receptionist were killed instantly. The receptionist's name was Edith Metzger, and that morning of August 11, 1956, when she woke up, she had no idea that a few hours later she would die in a car driven by Jackson Pollock. For years I did not know that these two events had occurred that same summer. But ever since I found out, at some point in my reading, I can hardly separate the two anymore. The summer of '56, Jackson Pollock died in a road accident, and I, Helen, took you, Frank, to Amsterdam, and gave you a room in my mother's house and, later, when you needed it, an entire studio, the room at the rear with the glass ceiling. You never thought about it as something I had given you. You never thought about any of that in terms of property or exchange. But the way I saw it, you were indebted to me, from the moment I ceremoniously placed the spare key in your cupped hands, the summer we were eighteen. And your debt, in my opinion, has only increased with all that has happened since.

AMSTERDAM

T he apartment was in the heart of Amsterdam and occupied the top three floors of a seventeenth-century
house, an era generally referred to as the Dutch Golden
Age. The Dutch historian Johan Huizinga has questioned,
however, this pompous borrowing of the term from Greek
mythology, a Golden Age when men and women were supposed to have lived in peace with the gods and nature. *If we
must give a name to our period of prosperity,* wrote Huizinga in
1941, *let us rather call it Wood and Steel, Pitch and Tar, Color
and Pigments, Boldness and Piety, Spirit and Imagination.*
Indeed it was, rather, an economic and cultural abundance,
due to urbanization, the political climate, and colonialism.
How could such a tiny country become one of the greatest
colonial powers of the seventeenth century? Who knows.
Moreover, Holland was, at the time, perhaps the only state in
Europe where wealth meant more than title, and where the
question of religious affiliation was held to be a private matter.
An interesting point in retrospect, the Dutch seventeenth century
also witnessed major revolutions in two domains: printing—
which, in its modern form, publishing, would become my pri-
mary activity; and painting, which would be yours. Painting
had always been quite important in the Netherlands—according to a census in 1560, there were already more painters in the
city of Antwerp than there were butchers, and a later calcula-
tion attributed five paintings to every two inhabitants. Dutch
pictorial art of the seventeenth century was characterized by its

iconoclasm, for the burghers who commissioned paintings wished to see themselves portrayed in their daily activities, both professional and domestic. Given the demand, painters became specialized: landscapes were the exclusive domain of van Goyen and Hobbema, whereas Jan Steen reigned over village satire the way Pieter de Hooch did over genre scenes. Heda painted exclusively *Ontbijtjes*, still lifes of breakfast tables, always containing the same objects; de Witte painted only monuments, and van de Velde only seascapes. Potter initially portrayed animals, then only calves; with d'Hondecoeter it was birds, with Wouwerman dappled horses, with van Beijeren seafood, and with Huysum, flowers. Most of these names are unfamiliar to us in the present day—but we worship Vermeer and Rembrandt, painters who sought to explore a variety of subjects and went totally unnoticed in their lifetime. The increase in the number of painters gave rise to a veritable artistic proletariat, and there were many artists who were forced to do other work while they practiced their art: van Ruisdael was a doctor, Jan Steen an innkeeper, van Goyen sold tulips, and Hobbema was a tax collector. No matter how you look at it, our house dated from an era that was blessed when it came to art and literature. It was tall, and beautiful, with large windows. The ground floor was occupied by a florist's, where you would, in years to come, buy me various bouquets to earn forgiveness for your equally varied transgressions. On the next floor were the kitchen, living room, and dining room, and there were two large rooms on each of the two upper floors. I took one room on the second and transformed the other into a study, and the top floor became your territory. This was the apartment where my mother had lived on her own in the short years preceding her marriage to my father. She had moved out virtually overnight, abandoning most of her belongings. So now we were living in her house. Her maiden name was still inscribed in gold letters on the letter box, *Maaike*

Helle, and every time I saw it when I went to fetch the mail, it gave me a shiver to think of the loveless woman who had brought me up. It was also in this apartment that my parents had decided to marry, or so I was told before I left Rome; and now that I in turn was living there, I would gaze every day with curiosity at the furniture that had witnessed that bad decision. I might, right from the start, have thought of my mother's apartment as an uninhabitable space—cursed, radioactive—but I didn't. I closed my eyes. I settled us both in, comfortably, and we lived there together for almost twenty years. Nowadays when I think back, I cannot help but conclude that, in one way or another, something of the place's bad luck did infect us after all.

Y ou took your correspondence course for roughly two months, according to my reckoning. You never re-sat the exam, but that hardly mattered. Horatio could very serenely go on telling people in Rome that you and I were studying in Holland, and no one could question him further about his son. I was, as anticipated, the perfect alibi. And besides, in your way you were studying. I hadn't told a complete lie: when you saw me working, you started working, too, although in the beginning it was probably just to pass the time. You didn't speak Dutch yet, you had to keep busy and, of course, you were still feeling somewhat bitter. You couldn't stand to see me busy and think that in comparison you might appear to be at loose ends. Those early weeks in Amsterdam, when I left you to start work, you tried at first to make me lose my focus, to tear me away from my desk by suggesting all sorts of promising activities, but I resisted, heroically. Then you tried another strategy—when you woke up at half past ten in the morning, and found me studiously going through my pile of books in the living room, you would sigh and smile and say, *Oh, poor you*, and go and lie down on a sofa where I could not fail to see you yawning irrepressibly, with your cup of coffee and a magazine. But I did not yield, as you must recall. I had fixed it so that you would get this far safe and sound and free, Frank. I never held it against you for having endangered our bid for freedom with your academic indolence, I had stuck up for you, I would have died for you, but I was not about to let you keep me from the studies I had dreamt of for so many years, studies which enthralled me, and which I was good at. It was as if the fact of having finally managed to leave my family home had filled me with energy: I immersed myself in my work with immense pleasure, I spent entire days at the library, and then nights reading; I felt as if I were in an empty clearing, this tidy, calm place that was my walnut desk in the room next to my bedroom. In that space, I filled page upon page with my passionate little handwriting. *What is a book?* I wrote. *What is a work? Why is a masterpiece a masterpiece?* My list of questions was endless, I was reading incredibly complicated books, in any of the languages I understood. I took notes, I tried to organize my thoughts, and when I went down to the kitchen to pour myself a glass of wine and butter some toast, to keep the interruption in my explorations as brief as possible, I would find you there, head bent close over your little piles of paper.

You had decided to become a genius. Sincerely interested, having no idea what lay in store in the years
ahead, I asked you what sort of genius—*I don't know*,
you replied cheerfully. *A total genius.* This was typical you, to
have thoughts like that. A genius in what field, I wanted to
know, with my usual serious attitude, but to you that didn't
matter. On scraps of paper you wrote and rewrote your ever-
changing schedules with no resolution in sight, you lined up
figures, did statistics, compared measurements. Every day you
jotted down a sentence and pinned it to the wall opposite your
desk, and every following morning you would cross it out to
write a new one. You feverishly sharpened your pencils, com-
piled reading lists, tore them up, started over. You didn't want
to be judged, you were surpassed by your own ambition, but
also very fragile, very precarious, very unhappy in your way; the
least little outside criticism could send you into a fit of rage,
because you yourself could see, only too well, that you were
getting nowhere. You had no back-up plan, you'd simply
planned to be a genius, you leafed through book after book to
attempt some research, to gather material, to become an
intellectual, someone brilliant, but nothing seemed to stick
intellectually, in spite of your efforts. You were using scissors
to hack at a substance that was too hard, too dense, a marble
that made you bend with effort. Nor did you really have a good
grasp of everyday life, although you actually did have a talent
for happiness, but all the details of practical life unsettled you,

as if no one had ever taken you backstage, behind the order of the world. No one had ever talked to you about maintenance. Only now have I actually worked it out: you were a man, you had grown up in embassies, and your mother, in her château in Paimpol, had servants, a cook, and a gardener. So everything was shocking, everything was disgusting, back in those days in Amsterdam when we were young and left to our own devices—the dishwater, sweeping the floor, peeling vegetables. You couldn't handle it, you were exasperatingly slow with any household chore, although you could run for two hours every morning along the frozen canals, singing. Real life depressed you. The day you turned twenty you wept all day because now you were too old to be taken for a child prodigy. And you were so young. We were both so young, that year. 1958. That autumn, Pius XII, the infamous pope who remained silent about the Holocaust, died in Castel Gandolfo. And you didn't want to work anymore, you said. But you had never even started, Frank. Your parents sent you money for your upkeep, and up to a point, I think that is also why you really only managed to start working when you were twenty-eight. *Art cannot be produced with the approval of one's parents*, I would write a few months later, at the top of my first essay. *Art is always something one does against everything, it is a luxury one offers oneself, never a leisure that others offer to us.*

Y ou were loafing about, and I was the opposite, doing nothing but working. That's all I've ever known how to do. It's true. Back then, however, I thought it would just be for a certain period of my life—I wanted to work hard while I was young and able. And besides, in the late 1950s it seemed an almost revolutionary thing to be doing, in an era when most young women wanted more than anything to get married, I wanted to work as hard as I could, fingers to the bone if need be, better than anyone. It was my greatest pride— but the years have passed, and now I must confess that no other period ever really came to replace that one—except, per- haps, the great decade when we lived together in Normandy, when I eased back somewhat from my literary occupations and learned a few new tangible skills—how to bake my own bread, plant beans, plan a cold-blooded murder—but subsequently, after our separation, I re-immersed myself even more deeply into intellectual work. That was my place in the world—the silent girl in a corner of the lecture hall, neck bent amidst the stacks in the libraries, little hand writing with a blue pen in the ever-present notebook; critical works, monographs, footnotes. And yet, despite the rigor of their argumentation, my books on the shelf, above the desk I have taken everywhere with me for forty years, my books tell of my personal questionings, my obsessions. I wrote all my books with the same serious approach, under pressure, first reading one book after another for months, often years, even, literally piling the volumes on my bed, with a pencil between my teeth, covering the lined pages of my notebooks, until at last, I would shut myself away in my study and write a hundred, or two hundred pages of dense prose, with almost no revision. Why did I do that? Now that I am entering my final years, for the first time I am seriously asking myself why. And all I recall is the intense pleasure of those days, those days shut in by myself, working, at night, during the day, and the excitement of the growing pile of pages, the thick stack of the last morning, the joy of having finished the work, then rereading, a cup of steaming coffee within reach, and then later, the printed cover, how silky it felt beneath my fingers. My entire life. Paper.

At university, not long after we arrived, I met someone. Erik was studying economics and he worked a few hours a week at the front desk of the university library. He had, as I would later realize, erroneously interpreted my enthusiasm for the place as being directed at him personally—he was convinced I was making a pass at him, while I was smiling giddily just to be holding my library card in my hand. He invited me to go out with him. Then, more from a lack of any real excuse not to be with him than because I really wanted it to, our romance began. With hindsight, I can see the part he played in my break-up with you—not really so much a *break-up* as the end of our physical relations. In Rome, we had been so isolated that the fact of being *together* had never really been questioned. But before long my relationship with Erik created barriers, as necessary as they were unexpected, within the life you and I shared, the life we'd always shared. I don't think I even tried to explain to him what I'd been through before—I probably just told him that I was the daughter of the British ambassador to Rome, and let him draw his own conclusions. Instead of telling him the truth about you and me—did I really even know it then, do I know it now?—I put the past behind me. But when he spent the night at the house I could hardly sleep, because of his nocturnal fidgeting, and because he snored. We were not close—after a year together we still did not know each other, never understood each other, had not changed a jot, had not taken a single step towards each other, we were still the girl who smiles in the stacks of the huge library and the boy who thinks the smile is for him. In the end, once I managed to extricate myself from my own lie, I returned with relief to the only life I really loved, the life I shared with you. I remember it well: on my way home, after I had just broken up with Erik in a coffee shop on the Negen Straatjes, walking in the drizzle and holding the little cardboard box that contained belongings of mine he had given back to me, and feeling so *good* in that moment as I closed the door behind me. I leaned for a moment against the wood to catch my breath, and without warning you appeared, a glass in your hand. For the entire duration of my affair you had said nothing, merely greeting Erik when you ran into him and nodding your head when I reminded you of his existence—but when you saw me that day and I told you it was all over, this time, you gave an almost imperceptible smile and said, laconically:

"Of course. Because that's not what love is about, Helen."

By the winter of 1959 we'd been living together for three years, and we would spend sixteen more years in the apartment in Amsterdam. Sometimes at night I heard noises coming from your room, and I could not work out whether you were weeping or making love. You were young, and enthusiastic, and desperately trying to find your way. It was during this period that you decided to take your ancient typewriter from the cupboard where you had stored it on arriving. You put it on the desk in your room, then you told me that from then on you were going to write novels. You locked yourself in, and when I would knock on the wooden door and tell you it was time to go shopping or to hang out the laundry, you would shout from within:

"I can't help you, sorry, I can't, Helen, I'm writing a book!"

It was a nightmare. At the time, I was trying to write a book which sought to record the turbulent emotions I felt when reading Thomas Hardy, and I wasn't having any luck, and you knew this very well, so your utter self-absorption in the middle of all this came across as pure provocation and was hurtful to me: it left me speechless. For weeks, I nevertheless put up with the humiliation you imposed on me; I took care of the house without you, walked alone through the snowy streets dragging our bags of shopping—you hadn't lost your appetite—scrubbed the bath, swept the stairs, washed the sheets and the dishes, remembered to buy tea, and cooked dinners for our friends. I was full of empathy towards Mrs. Tolstoy and Mrs.

Freud and Mrs. Marx and all the others. And I was going *mad*. I couldn't write anymore. I did not have a second to myself, and I could no longer make any noise in my own house. You had locked yourself in your room like some ferocious bear I lived in dread of rousing from his long hibernation. You explained that you had decided to write every day from nine in the morning until eight o'clock at night, you had worked out the average number of words in a masterpiece, then the average number of words you could type per minute, and then you'd calculated the time it would take for you to write your book if you maintained this pace. I hated your idea, I hated your book, and I was so angry with you for making me hate a book. My anger made me cruel, and when you took a break to come and join me for lunch, I would ask you, casual as can be, how you were getting on—weren't you a bit frightened of rushing into such a project, did you suffer from writer's block at all, what exactly did you think about in the morning when you sat down to work, what were you hoping to gain from the entire project, anyway, you weren't expecting to become a writer—or were you? Hadn't you bitten off more than you could chew?

Y ou didn't say anything. You occasionally shivered slightly, but it was December, after all, and you didn't say anything. You had never been so withholding with me before. You literally slipped through my fingers. When I asked you in a detached tone of voice whether I could read what you had written, you said *no*.

"Of course," I said, "I can wait until you've finished."

"No," you said softly, not looking at me. "Never, Helen. You are never going to read my book. You would be far too critical, and I don't want your opinion."

I made fun of you. I told you that the first thing everyone must learn when writing was to accept criticism, to learn to take it, even to anticipate it, and it was ridiculous to sit off in one's corner writing any old rubbish and then caress it like a masterpiece without ever sharing it with others or giving anyone the chance to form an opinion.

"It's not ridiculous at all," you replied. "You have your vision of literature, I have mine, and that's it. You don't have a monopoly on writing, because no such thing exists. You're jealous because I'm writing a book. If that's really your thing, why aren't you writing your own book?"

I became obsessed with the idea of reading the book you claimed to be writing under my nose. I spied on your comings and goings to the bathroom, hoping to slip into your room while you were in the shower, but you had locked the door. For a full month, you didn't leave the apartment. Every day, all day long, you stayed locked in your room. Your lunch break was carefully timed. At last one afternoon, you went out at three o'clock, not saying where you were going. The moment I saw through the window that you had turned the street corner, I went to try your door. To my astonishment it wasn't locked. I went in. I saw the neatly made bed, with your patterned duvet, the posters on the wall, the little shelf of books, and on the desk, the typewriter, gleaming, threatening, the focus of my sleepless nights. I went closer. There was a page on the platen. I leaned closer to read what was there, and the last word typed at the bottom of the page was my first name. Frank, do you remember what you wrote?

When I met you
I had never
Loved anyone yet.
Nor had you.
And you still haven't.
All your love
Has melted like snow in sunlight
Into your work
So I try to work
And to understand you, Helen.

T hat, to my knowledge, is the only poem you ever wrote. I tore the sheet from the typewriter that day, because it was clearly meant for me, so obviously a message addressed to me, a delivery staged like some lesson to teach me who I was. We never spoke about it. I took the poem and went out before you came back, and the following day you stopped locking yourself in your room, stopped talking about writing a book. I never found out what you had done, exactly, during those four weeks alone in your room for which I made you pay so dearly. That poem is your only poem, and now that I think of it, standing here across from you in London, because a spot of ink on the nail of your middle finger suddenly reminded me of your erstwhile writerly ambitions, it gives me shivers to think that that folded sheet of paper is only a few streets away, hidden at the back of my wardrobe in the Hartmann Tresore safe, a safe which contains nothing else.

PAINTING

C harlie, one of my former classmates, had stopped coming to class a few months earlier, but we still saw him now and then, because he lived in our neighborhood and was trying to seduce me. One day he invited us for a drink in the late afternoon, and there were huge sheets of newspaper spread all over the floor, because Charlie was standing on a ladder repainting a wall, with one brush in his hand and another between his teeth. As soon as we arrived he came down off his ladder to prepare us a hot drink, and we chatted for a long time, standing in his kitchen—a real shambles—holding our cups of tea.

"Charlie, what's that smell?" you asked him after a while.

"It's the paint," replied Charlie with a shrug.

"The paint," you echoed.

Have I attached too much importance to that moment? I don't know. But ever since, I've firmly believed that it was, in part, from that moment on that everything fell into place for you. I've never forgotten how your face suddenly lit up, interested, relaxed. I remember how surprised Charlie was that you hadn't immediately recognized the characteristic smell of fresh paint, but in a way, he was mistaken: you may have been incapable of guessing the nature of what you were smelling, but you had indisputably *recognized* the paint as something that was mysteriously meant for you, and had reacted to it at once. You didn't say anything to me, not a word, as we walked home along the canals, but the subject certainly had not left you, the thought had made its way into your mind like the scent wafting into your nostrils. In the weeks and months that followed, a new kind of smile came to bloom on your face, a half smile, both fierce and very calm, and I often wanted to ask you about it, but something held me back, as if there were something so private about it that even I did not dare bring it up. I would think about it at night as I drifted off, astonished that I had let yet another day go by without mentioning it to you, but I could not find the words, I did not know how to frame my question—*what is this new smile all about?*—and by morning I had forgotten about it. The days went by. To be honest, I was very busy myself at the time: in addition to the various translations I was working on, I was writing a piece for an academic volume I'd collaborated on, about the first use of copyright. Time was rushing by, and I must have been sincerely relieved to sense that you were busy and content, after all these years of torment. You no longer stayed at home pacing back and forth like some caged beast; you went out, you would leave the house before I was even awake, and you came back only late at night, eyes shining, while you went on smiling, inexplicably.

What you were doing all that time was something I could only guess at or work out much later: I believe you had set off on a quest to learn about painting, not exactly sure what you were looking for, but buoyed by the certainty that you would find it wherever painting was also to be found. And Amsterdam, in the 1960s, was a good place for that. I imagine you must have gone to the Rijksmuseum, to the Stedelijk, to the Rembrandt House, and you must have talked about painting with people around you, probably with Charlie at first, and I imagine Charlie failed to see what you were after, so you went elsewhere for the answers to your tireless questions—antique shops, art-supply shops, the street, cafés, you must have talked to everyone you met and let yourself bounce off their ideas, followed the thread all the way to the Rijksakademie van beeldende kunsten, the State Academy of Fine Arts, and from there, step by step, to the Kunstnijverhei-dsonderwijs, the Institute of Applied Art, where you met Theo Soto-Salinas and Ossip Gang, who were both students there in 1966. You never studied at either of those institutions, despite claims to the contrary, but you hung out in the neighborhood bars and at the little exhibition galleries, and that was how you got to know Soto and Gang, and many others whose names have not found their place in the great history of art. It was thanks to them that you were able to study after all, *in absentia*, so to speak, or contumaciously, rather, since the word *contumacy* comes from the Latin word for *spirit of independence, obstinacy, stubbornness,* but also *pride*—and years later, when the time for glory had arrived, your arrogance would remain intact when you asserted that, of the three of you, only you had never belonged to any school. Perhaps it is my own temperate nature that has inspired this opinion, but personally I never believed that either Gang or Soto *belonged* to any school at all—they had simply studied somewhere, and besides, they were younger than we were, and better at everything than you were when you met them. Unwittingly, they gave you an education, by repeating over a pint of beer in the evening what they'd learned in class during the day, and by showing you their tools, introducing you to their friends, and by opening the doors to their world for you, they trained you. Later, your ingratitude towards them always seemed misguided to me, a lack of manners, but you would probably counter, even today, that a lack of manners is meaningless, in comparison to creative genius.

Yet you do owe them a great deal. I remember the first evening you brought them home, those two lively, intelligent young men, with their hands callused from the strain of working with chisel and sandpaper, and they were famished—something you never mentioned later, along with everything else, when you compared yourself to them; you never mentioned how poor they'd been, how their parents had paid for their admission fees and for lodgings that were just barely decent, but gave them only a few guilders a month for their room and board, but I remember those starving young men with their emaciated cheeks. I remember, Frank. I haven't forgotten a thing. Even if you were gifted, as time has amply proven, your expertise at painting was not heaven-sent. You worked hard—simply, you worked in the shadows, and I suspect you destroyed all your first sketches as if to erase the history of your failed attempts, to give the impression that you were already incredibly skilled from the very start. I often thought that in the beginning you suffered from some sort of complex with regard to Ossip and Soto, who had learned to paint much earlier, and that this was why you covered your tracks so carefully, in order to come out on top by asserting that this was not your vocation but an inherent gift, rather, discovered late in the day; that was the only argument still available to you. There might be a certain charm to producing awkward but already striking drawings from childhood, but to offer similar preliminary sketches to the eyes of the world at the age of twenty-eight shows an indisputable lack not only of panache but above all of lucidity. You were not always brilliantly perceptive, but it must be said that once you got started in your career as an artist—your first and only career—you did things stylishly, like any good son of a diplomat. You toiled in utter secrecy, sneaking your art supplies into the house without me even knowing; you spied on your best friends, never letting any of your intentions show—I am convinced that in the beginning, for months, even, Soto and Ossip and all the others they introduced you to did not have the slightest idea of what you were planning, and no doubt they saw you as just some young man, a bit older than they were, who was at sufficiently loose ends to tag along to private viewings and give them a hand with odd jobs. But all that time, you were learning: the jargon, the materials, the ceramics, the mixtures, the history, the mythology of art; you bought them drinks with your father's money, but you were the one who was drinking in their teachings, you were the one who *desired,* in the whole business. They didn't see you coming. Nor did I.

I must admit I don't know anything about your actual apprenticeship. I was never given the slightest report on your first sketches or botched attempts. As I said, I was busy with my books, and you must have found the perfect time slots to work well away from my gaze, because for months I did not suspect a thing. I thought you went out, and came home late, that you had made new acquaintances and were sharing things with them—we had been living together for ten years by then, and I didn't shadow you—you had your life, and I had mine. I'd played big sister to you for long enough, and I was tired of it, I had other priorities. Seven years earlier, when you had wanted to shut yourself out of sight to write your novel, it had seemed unbearable to me, but I thought the poem that had emerged from that time had cured me, to a degree, of my worse inclinations and helped me grow up. I was leading a rich and fascinating life by then, a life I had built and which I was proud of, and I knew how to be happy for others. To be sure, to see you captivated by something relieved me of the guilt I sometimes felt at the thought I was leaving you by the wayside. I think my contentment at putting in good work made me more generous. From time to time I met Ossip and Soto and all the others in our living room, and I saw books and papers and sketchbooks piling up in the corridor outside your room, but I paid no attention, I did not realize what it meant. I was simply glad that you seemed to have found something to do, whatever it might be. Sometimes I heard you talking loudly through the door, listening to music while you smoked; I saw people coming in the house laden with heavy bags, then afterwards for days you might be gone altogether. I would worry, but you always showed up again eventually and shut yourself up in your room as usual. Everything was fine. You told me nothing about your new life, but there were nights when we came back together, slightly drunk, and we kissed in the stairs leading up to our hideout and made love on the immaculate floor of my mother's apartment. Sometimes, too, when we came home even later, in the early morning hours, the fragrance of hot milk with honey would be floating all over Amsterdam with the arrival of the cargo ships—only much later did I learn that this odor was due to the huge shipments of soy they transported. Do you remember? We thrilled to the sugary smell, as we opened the front door, young, over-excited, and settled onto the mattress in the living room to doze hand in hand until one of us had the strength to get up and make the morning coffee and start the day. I don't know why it wasn't more complicated than that at the time—perhaps, simply, because we were innocent.

You began to paint. With my consent, you moved into the big room to the north, because it had a sort of glass ceiling. The apartment began to smell of turpentine, a smell I loved, and you became both calmer and more vibrant. You seemed to have given up sleeping, you were covered in splotches of paint, and not a sound came from your room when I went to put my ear against the door. One day you opened it all of a sudden and found me there, and I stumbled into your arms. I was about to make an excuse, but you exclaimed:

"Here you are! I was about to come and get you! Come have a look!"

And you pulled me by the arm into the room where, for the first time, I saw your first painting. The paint was still wet, the image not quite finalized, but everything was there, the blues and gold, the reds, deep blacks, and the precision, and the sheer size of it, which held me spellbound that time as it would every time thereafter. How to find the words to say what it meant to me, to open a door in my own home and come upon a thing like that. The canvas literally absorbed space, it was all you saw, we stood in front of it but we were also inside it, engulfed. I thought of cherry trees in bloom in the April frost, when in the space of a few hours a tree scatters a thick pink carpet to the ground; I felt like one of those cherry trees. I was flabbergasted, and you stood next to me, you had picked up a cup of cold coffee and were lighting a cigarette, observing me, not so much to see my reaction but to enjoy it to the fullest, because you knew very well what you had just done. You had succeeded in making the contents of your mind visible to the world. You had succeeded in making yourself heard. We stayed by the painting all day. I knew it was the end of one thing and the beginning of something else, but I don't know whether you yourself knew this. When night fell, we lit candles and stayed there, not speaking, playing backgammon and drinking wine in silence, occasionally glancing over at the canvas next to us, as if it were a sleeping animal. I shall never forget it, Frank.

What happened in the days that followed? I cannot recall, I think you stayed in your room, but I no longer sensed the characteristic vibration of painting through the door, and when I ran into you making coffee in the kitchen, your clothes were immaculate. You went around with a constant stack of books piled in your arms like firewood, you seemed to be accumulating them in your room, but sometimes I saw you go out with them as well, and then come back, and I did not know where you had been in the interim. During your absences, I would go into your room and gaze at the painting, unconsciously, no doubt, to make sure it hadn't moved, hadn't left us, as if I knew somehow that everything would change the moment the frame went through the door. I sometimes gauged its size at a quick glance, and became almost convinced that it would be impossible, in any case—the stretcher bars seemed too wide for even the slightest hope of getting the canvas down our steep, narrow staircase. There were times I was afraid that you might saw it into pieces in order to get it out, but I was mistaken. In fact, as you explained when the day eventually did come, you had carefully calculated the size of the canvas, basing it on the width of the corridor and the stairs, and had crafted with your own hands the biggest stretcher frame that could squeeze through the space allotted. The canvas fit exactly within the limits of our dwelling. But I did go on to share my concern with you, my fear that you might saw this marvel in half, and much later, years later, that is exactly what you did. Yes, a day would come when you felt you no longer belonged in a house, and you painted canvases that were even more beautiful, then went on to mutilate them with a saber saw in order to take them out into the damp street one after the other; you were dead drunk, utterly indifferent, and totally unaware of the wound you were inflicting upon yourself. These canvases are worth a fortune nowadays, most of them sleeping in the vaults or private studies of the powerful—who, unsurprisingly, are aroused by the sight of destruction, so that only a few of these works have been acquired by museums, and whenever I come across one of them, turning the corner between two exhibition rooms, I feel a twinge of anguish. Now and again I happen without warning upon one of the canvases from this late period, forcefully reassembled by some maniacal curator wielding a staple gun, and it's like seeing a bearskin in front of a fireplace, open-jawed and forever silenced, and at times like that I can't help but think that it is all my fault. I could have prevented it, and I did anything but, I gave the impetus to the carnage, all those years ago. Experts agree in saying that this was perhaps the most innovative work of the era, the result of your great audacity, a stroke of genius, but it was our life. It was your life, Frank. You were the one who was being dismantled at the time, you were the one who was sawn in two, cleaned out, undone. And I was to blame.

You produced other paintings, and still more paintings. One day Charlie came and said he'd like to be your agent, even though he had never, of course, been anyone's agent before. But since that day when we went to his place and you had your epiphany, he had been fascinated by what you were doing, he followed you everywhere, and told people how you'd discovered painting because of him. Ossip and Soto-Salinas listened to him very kindly. People came and went in the apartment, and one day you gathered everyone there, and you set about taking the paintings from the studio to move them to the gallery where Charlie, against all expectations, had just landed you your first contract. It was a medium-sized gallery on the corner of two streets in De Pijp. And there, on a Thursday in October, 1966, you sold your first painting. The exhibition had been on for three weeks, and you never left the place, probably because you knew that it was actually you that was for sale. That Thursday, a man came into the gallery, he must have been in his forties, and he was—we found this out later—the widower of a very wealthy old woman, who herself had been the widow of an even older very wealthy man, and she had taken this younger man as her second husband the moment the final nail had been driven into the first husband's coffin. He had been her secretary or something like that. He walked around looking at the walls, with an expression like some deep-water fish. He didn't pay the slightest attention to your work, and when he spoke to you, it was to ask whether the gallery had any paintings by Geer van Velde. You replied that you were not the gallery owner, but the artist, and he recoiled as if he had been stung. He must have dreaded the possibility that some minor artist with too much time on his hands might dig his claws into him and not let go, but at that very moment, as if by magic, the owner came up from the cellar and began to sing your praises, saying that you were one of the freshest and most innovative artists she had. She began chatting with the client in a jargon we were not yet familiar with, but which we would soon add to the list of foreign languages we could speak, and eventually the man went closer to your paintings to take a better look, and asked if it was really you who had painted this. You nodded, and the man asked if you had anything else and you said *yes* again, and when the man wanted to know whether you had already sold anything, you said *no*, in a tone where perhaps only I could detect a touch of annoyance and regret, but against all expectations, this was apparently the appropriate sequence of terse replies, because the man came out and said he wanted one of your paintings, on the spot, that he would leave with it that very day, as soon as the check was signed, and he wanted *you* to choose the painting for him. Very slowly you got up off your stool— this measured slowness was a real effort, I thought, on your part, normally so wild—to gaze attentively at your own canvases.

"For someone like you," you said at last, pointing to the smallest canvas, twelve by twelve square, "I can think only of this one."

The man made a face, because it was as if, at that very moment, his entire self-image had been reduced to the size of the canvas you were allotting to him, and a small format seemed unworthy. His voice was downright beseeching when he said:

"This one, really? I was thinking something more—"

You immediately broke in, warmly: "You are a connoisseur. You're right, of course. What was I thinking? No, what you need, the right thing for you, has to be this one."

And you led him over to a canvas that was twice as big, a sort of still life of your desk from very close up: trapped in the paint one could make out cinema tickets, confetti, and scribbled sheets of paper, all submerged under broad strokes of dark blue paint, the rough seas of your private life, an extremely moving picture, I thought, but also very conventional—Braque and Picasso were already making collages like this at the turn of the century—and once again, the man made a face.

"I don't know," he said. "Isn't it a bit . . . ? I don't know," he said again. "I can pay any price. I would just like to buy your best work."

And so you led him around from painting to painting for perhaps a quarter of an hour, following an itinerary that seemed to have been worked out in advance. You gave him a tour of the entire gallery, going so far as to compare your work with that of other artists on display; you underlined their qualities, the better to promote your own, and in the end, you took the buyer up to your most colossal, most expensive painting. Only then did the man seem satisfied, and I thought, with my usual cool-headed approach: *All he wanted was the biggest one, we should have known from the start.* But your little performance did have its purpose: you'd managed to muddle the man's thoughts, to such a degree that by the time he had reached a certain point, he didn't want to buy just one painting, but all of them—because the thought of leaving a single one behind made him ill, from some superstition, or that since the artist himself had shown them all to him, this made him feel they all belonged to him.

"I'll take them all," he had said, adding with an embarrassed laugh: "I'll have made today worth your while."

"But you can't," you replied. "You can't, you cannot just buy everything. Imagine, I wouldn't have anything left."

You had wound the buyer up in a skein of absurd, incomprehensible phrases, delivered with a growing vehemence that gradually caused him to back down, as if intimidated, and he finally considered himself lucky to come away with the large-format canvas he had seen last of all, and which was the only one you would let him have. In the days that followed, a frenetic crowd—and we never knew whether they had been sent by the first buyer or simply heard that a new painter had arrived on the scene—came to see and buy the paintings for themselves, too, so that by the end of the week there was not a single one left. You had sold your paintings practically non-stop for three weeks, constantly raising the price, telling your stories, perfecting your act in your artist-in-dungarees get-up until you had completely emptied your studio of all it contained. And basically, Frank, all of that had been possible because you were a good diplomat, not because you were a good artist.

I f I am to believe what is written in your biography, to this
day no one knows what you did in the weeks that followed
your first miraculous sale—but I do know. You took me to
Italy. You took me home. You booked the tickets without
breathing a word of it to me, and the day after the exhibition
ended, early in the morning, you told me to pack my case, and
we set off, just like that. We flew first to Rome, where we spent
two nights wandering around our favorite streets, sleeping
during the day, and then from there you hired a car, and we
drove north along the coast through all of Tuscany. We would
stop at roadside *alberghi* and sleep with the windows wide
open. It was like being children again, although our parents
had never taken us to those places, but we rediscovered our
Italian tête-à-têtes, the language of our common ground—*Mi
capisci?*—and the food we loved, and the burning sun we had
missed all those chilly years in Holland. It was something I had
never imagined, something that was deeply strange and foreign: going on holiday. At one point during the trip we rented
a house for a week, a house that was completely isolated amid
fields of almond trees, and we did nothing, you hadn't even
brought a sketchbook with you, we simply sat on the stone terrace drinking aniseed aperitifs while we peeled fruit with a
knife, reminiscing about our childhood, and at night we made
love. Over, and over, and over. We had not made love for years,
but in Italy, in the month of May, 1967, that was all we did for
an entire week. I didn't think. It was so familiar. And besides,

I was bursting with pride for your sake, stunned by what you had accomplished over the last few months, this metamorphosis, not only your success, but also your adherence to the notion of effort. At last you had joined me in the arena, and I spread out my arms to you. During the day, we drove around the sun-drenched countryside for hours, me with my feet up on the dash, you bare-chested in your shorts and trainers. We visited churches, bought wine, bit passionately into raw tomatoes, alone on earth. I didn't want it to end, ever.

The very evening of our return we went out for drinks with the whole gang. You began to flirt with a dark-haired girl, a stranger to me, and in the end you brought her home, because she had nowhere to stay. I had work to finish the next day, and I went to bed before the two of you. In the morning, I was in bed writing when you burst into my room, clearly agitated, hair disheveled, and wearing your characteristic hungover look. You were so handsome to me. I thought that you wanted to make love to me in the early morning sunlight. But you said:

"You have to help me, Helen."

"To do what?"

"To get rid of the girl from last night. I don't even know her name. But there's another girl arriving any minute, and she mustn't see her, because this one's the love of my life."

At a certain point the love of your life might, rather, be the one who helps you get out of scrapes like this, I thought bitterly, but I held my tongue. I did not say a word. I put on my coat and went to invite the girl from last night for a drink. The girls who slept with you always wanted to spend time with me afterwards, no doubt to make sure that I was not your partner; perhaps, too, with the realistic hope that my blessing might secure their position. This girl must have sensed this, too, because she immediately followed me. In a nearby café I listened distractedly as she told me who she was, laying her cards on the table in hopes that I would tell you about her, and while she was babbling on, I was thinking of the two of us in Italy, about what we had done, what we had said to one another. Once I had managed to bring the conversation to an end, I went home alone along the canals, full of joy at the thought of seeing you, so happy that I forgot *why* I had left the house one hour earlier. When I went in the house I climbed the stairs four by four, and you and Anna were just getting dressed, laughing where you stood next to my sink.

I realized at that moment that I had fallen passionately in love with you, Frank Appledore. When I had you, I didn't keep you, and now, I was no longer with you, and my rights had ceased to prevail over anything else. Yet I had been under the impression that something had happened between us in Italy, I believed you had felt it, too, and that my feelings had been reciprocated—but apparently, I was mistaken. At no time did you want to hurt me. You simply hadn't guessed what I was feeling, because I hadn't said anything about it. And this was how Anna slipped into our lives.

Anna

nnelieke van Opstall—Anna. Thirty-three the year we
met her. Daughter, granddaughter, and sister of Dutch
industrialists, a dynasty in the metallurgical sector.
With the money from an inheritance, she had opened an art
gallery. That was how you met her: she'd seen your paintings
somewhere and contacted you to suggest you work with her
from then on. She was tall, beautiful, self-assured—for you, it
was love at first sight. I am not casting the first stone. Anna
offered you the security and dignity you would not have found
on your own, and which I don't think I was capable of offering you—I could make you sandwiches for lunch, I could wash
and fold your laundry, I could ring your mother for you, but I
could not prepare the battlefield for you to conquer the art
world. Anna could. She introduced you to influential people,
rich people, intelligent people, she brought you into the circles
that would ensure your survival for years to come, she legit-
imized you. When you entered a room together, hand in hand,
all heads turned to Annelieke, and when they had at last finished inspecting her, they looked at you, too, because her bril-
liance instantly illuminated you, like the night-time lights of a
monument. Everyone wanted to know your secret, to know
who you were, this man who had managed to capture such a
trophy woman. People apparently had no end of questions
regarding your relationship and your private life, so when they
found out you were an artist they all wanted to see your paintings, and as soon as they'd seen them they were desperate to

100 - JULIA KERNINON

have them. It was almost magical. If you wanted to sell a few paintings, all you had to do was show up at a private viewing with Annelieke, and that very evening your telephone was constantly ringing, and while you were with her, drinking rum and ignoring your calls, all the local art lovers wanted to come to your house and visit your studio. You told me that there were times, after a dinner, when you discovered a painting had disappeared from the living room or the corridor, because people literally took everything—even, more than once, paintings that were not by you, when they found nothing better. Annelieke was the best agent you could've had, in those years, and to this day she remains one of the finest experts on your work. In the four years you were together, she was unmatched when it came to winning over a reticent curator, or finding a vehicle to transport your canvases, or keeping you to your impossible schedule, or standing in for you at the last minute when you were drunk and stubborn and refused to show up for appointments. She was made for it. But I tend to think that you never completely accepted this brilliant side of hers, that you remained jealous of it, even though you were its prime beneficiary. There was too much personality in your relationship, too much beauty, too much energy, too many shared interests as well. At one point, you no longer wanted to share, you no longer wanted to be part of the Frank-and-Annelieke duo, you were fed up with all the compliments you received, tired of being part of a team, tired of your companion's charm overshadowing your artistic production, tired of not being able to tell where one ended and the other began, tired of hearing the husky laughter of a tall, powerful woman ringing out at your exhibitions.

But I'm getting ahead of myself. Let me backtrack. 1967. You were in love. You were rich. You wasted no time in moving in with Annelieke into an eight-room bourgeois apartment: you chose it for a big room with four windows overlooking the Amstel river, which you wanted to have as your studio. You installed huge oak shelving, made to order, all the way to the ceiling, to store all your materials—paints, brushes of all sizes, papers, canvases, frames, sponges, pigments, solvents, scissors, brand-new knives, and a desk you had designed yourself. You talked about it to everyone, you invited people to come and see your perfect set-up. Your sudden passion for interior decoration made me think of Honoré de Balzac, and I smiled in silence. To be sure, you had a studio—but in actual fact you came back to our apartment every day to work. In a way, we continued sharing our lives—you up on the top floor, painting, me in my study writing, running into each other by the coffee pot like before. Nothing had changed, for us—except that we had become liars.

"But we grew up with liars," you said, "didn't we? That was practically all we knew. Liars, cheats, opportunists, crooks. My parents. Your parents. No? We never knew anything else."

And yet I regularly tried to raise the subject with you, probably deep down more to ease my own mind than to make you change yours. I got on well with Anna. I liked her very much. I didn't want to offend her. In a cowardly way, I didn't want her to suspect me of anything, I was trying so hard not to be jealous anymore, I wanted everything to go well, and this daily lie worried me, but you said, "Honestly, Helen, what is the worst thing that could happen, in your opinion? The worst thing is that I will confess to her that I cannot leave my first studio, that I'm superstitious, that it's good for both of us, *e basta*. What could she possibly say to that?"

But of course, it wasn't that simple—one way or another, your room, left intact in my apartment, gave you a reason to be secretive and dishonest, and you got used to your clandestine life. It would take you years, but of course in the end you found something besides painting to justify your interest in this perfect lie. It was as if you were drifting away, little by little, until never again would you be able to admit openly where you were, or even, perhaps, to know it yourself for certain. One day when I went sailing I learned that if you are off course by so much as one degree, you will head off at a diagonal in the wrong direction and be lost forever. I think that is what you did, Frank.

Of course, our secret arrangement was only partly responsible for your dissipation; the main cause was painting. From the start, you immersed yourself in painting the way one immerses oneself in the countryside or in darkness, the way one goes through the curtain of a waterfall from a cave to the outside, or rather, in this case, from the outside into the unfathomable depths of the cave. You went into painting, in the strictest sense of the term, and in a way, you never came out again. Even though you had got there by chance, after numerous failures in other fields, you turned out to be more yourself, there, than ever before, and this also meant you acquired new, multiple personas. The mere contact with art made your personality blossom in a literally spectacular way. I watched the sensitive young man I'd known become a man with ravishing charisma, a tireless conversationalist, but sometimes I also caught a glimpse of the flip side of this metamorphosis—while you were becoming a personality, the worker in you was constantly increasing the distance separating him from the world, like an animal relentlessly patrolling its den in wide circles, the better to protect it. If you came to paint at my place, back then, it was, first of all, because you knew you would be sheltered from curious gazes, and also because you felt a need to isolate your overflowing existence—on one side of the Amstel, life in public, your worldly, conjugal life with Annelieke, evenings of grand extravagance, drinking pink champagne; on the other, the almost academic calm of our long association, the possibility of having no one to see to besides oneself and which, in your opinion, was the condition *sine qua non* of artistic practice. We worked in the apartment where we'd been young, together and separately. I sometimes felt as if we were pioneers arriving in undiscovered territory, that we'd spent our twenties carefully choosing a terrain, leveling the soil, then erecting the building where we would live and create, and only now could we really get down to work, after all this patient preparation. It was hard for me to say when my studies had ended—after completing my degree course at university, I went on to study literature on a professional basis, writing reviews and articles, editing anthologies, organizing symposia. No more heading to campus with my leather briefcase. I settled in my little study first thing in the morning, in my pajamas. With the money I had patiently put aside from the subsidies my father sent me, and without mentioning it to anyone, I'd just founded a literary review and a little publishing house, and you were painting like a madman, but you had apparently not completely lost your passion for the written word, and so sometimes instead of painting, you would join me in the living room to help me read the articles that were submitted for publication, and you made subtle collages for the cover illustrations, without ever agreeing to sign them. You went with me to the printer's, rummaging through everything, opening drawers and boxes, breathing in lungfuls of ink, carrying bundles of galleys and crates of paper, relieved, I think, to be able to find a temporary refuge as a jack-of-all-trades. You were already well known, although not as much as today of course, but all the same, your face appeared regularly in specialized reviews, and it was public knowledge that Frank Appledore lived in Amsterdam, yet no one ever seemed to recognize you during our outings. The printer and his workers, the odd hack who came to drop off a text, all addressed you as if you were no more than some passing stranger, my brother, perhaps, or a distant cousin, tagging along in my wake by chance, but without any particular merit of your own. I was careful not to say anything, but I was stunned. I don't know if you meant for it to stop one day—whether you knew that in the near future there would come a time when you would no longer be able to switch off your schizophrenia like a neon light, or that over time people would learn to recognize you no matter the circumstance. A day would come when all sanctuary would be lost, all inner and outer peace. People would recognize you beneath your sadness and despair, they would no longer need your strategic diversions to call attention to you in the street. Sometimes you would even be spotted in places where you were not—something about a stranger's shape or accent would cause others to take him for you, and the murmur of the crowd would relentlessly repeat your name, like a litany.

B ut that was much later. First of all, there came 1971 and 1972, when you worked frenetically. You got up early in the morning, in your room with its inlaid wooden floor, gobbled down two bowls of cereal one after the other using the van Opstalls' hundred-year-old porcelain, then you slipped on a T-shirt, a woolen jumper, and a pair of stained trousers, and walked from your house to mine. (I see you again as a young man, walking or riding your bike through the streets of Amsterdam, with your ever-present mottled gray jumpers, your pea jacket and the thick woolen socks that I bought for you by the dozen at De Bijenkorf.) On the way, you often stopped off at a street stall to order two rollmops and a little bottle of schnapps, and there were times when you were so deeply immersed in your painting, already thinking about what you had done the day before, that you did not even stop to greet me on your way up the stairs to your hideout. I would hear the creak of the wooden stairs and, sitting at my desk on the third floor, turn my head just in time to catch a glimpse of your shoe or back disappearing furtively towards the floor above. During those years I watched you expand until you became someone who was very different from the person I'd known before. Whether it was subconscious or deliberate, in the end you had chosen the hardest career, that of an artist, but, mysteriously, you seemed to excel at it. People stood patiently in the street outside a gallery to come and get a closer look at you—how splendid you were, just thirty-four, victorious. Above your desk you had pinned a sentence by Reverdy about Picasso, and which said: *He decided to take no account of the huge mass of knowledge and experience he had acquired, and he summoned himself to start everything all over again.* You certainly did not have Picasso's experience—you had been painting for less than six years, whereas the Picasso Reverdy was referring to, the Picasso who was about to paint *Les Demoiselles d'Avignon,* had, at the age of only twenty-seven, a technical expertise and intimate knowledge of painting that was undoubtedly far superior to your own. And what you did, in fact, was the exact opposite of what the Spanish master had set about doing: as you basically did not know a great deal, you proceeded to learn how to paint. You had made a dazzling, spectacular entry into the art world, but it did not take you long to see your coronation as a sort of misunderstanding, an imposture. From that moment on, your satisfaction on hearing praise would be transformed into scorn towards those who uttered it.

And so, you came back to the house, every day, like a freeloader. When you weren't painting, you read books about painting. You would curl up in an armchair in the living room to read and jot down the things you liked on little squares of paper.

Painting is sometimes like those recipes where you do all manner of elaborate things to a duck, and then end up putting it on one side and only using the skin.
Lucian Freud

It was capital. It was as if it were the work of an entire civilization, not just one man.
Willem de Kooning speaking of his discovery of the work of Alberto Giacometti

People exist only insofar as I can drink with them.
Amedeo Modigliani

Do you think I would have painted this crap if I knew how to draw a hand?
Jackson Pollock

You adored Pollock, and at the same time he made you so angry. You said his process was very detrimental to painting as an art, throwing paint like that onto the canvas, while he let himself be filmed, dear God, filmed while he did it. Now everyone thought paint was something that was meant to be thrown, whereas he was the only one who could do it right. Andy Warhol angered you for the same reasons, or almost, but Malevich didn't, because in your opinion he had set a precedent, and that was more important. You loved modern art more than anything, even de Staël, who you said was such a bad painter in his early years, when he was still trying to do something he was not cut out to do—and then he went on to produce such dazzling work, the way his landscapes, if you looked at them closely, seemed completely abstract, whereas if you took a few steps back, suddenly you saw everything—the hill, the tree, the valley, the emotion. And yet you liked Franz Kline very much, too—because you could see the movement, the brush strokes, and this was important, too, and it simply moved you. And then there was Francis Bacon, who had provided the answer once and for all to the question of how to paint human beings, which profile to favor: neither. To paint someone, you explained, you had to paint them in their entirety, in motion, in doubt. Because that was what made up a human being. As for you, well, you wanted to draw a hand. Not reinvent it, not *endanger reality* in your art, not bring about *a revolution in the image* or that sort of rubbish—but paint a hand, paint it perfectly, academically, like Raphael, Leonardo, Titian. You said you wanted to know how to paint feet, legs, shoes—and paint landscapes properly, with true colors, with perspective. Everyone had forgotten what painting was about in the beginning, you said proudly, for all that you'd only been painting for six years. You were fed up with ending up at exhibitions where the visual artists stood on boxes and recited bad poetry, then knelt down to shove the boxes along with their forehead as they crawled forward on all fours and eventually lay on the floor like idiots, while everyone around them wondered whether it was over or not, whether it was time to applaud, was the buffet open, could they leave now. I listened to you, fascinated. You were becoming a new person: determined, fierce, biased. I placed my head in your lap and closed my eyes, and I listened to you telling me about your vision of work.

You probably don't know this, but I went on seeing Anna after the two of you separated. Not just the months immediately afterwards—I saw her all my life. I never lost touch with her. We were friends, of course, but that is not the only reason. In fact, we had been enemies—I have never been able to erase your two laughing faces in the bathroom at Prinsenstraat from my memory. You have surely forgotten, but Anna hadn't, she took me by surprise when she said, not long after you separated, *On a certain level you are glad, Helen, and we both know it.* And she was not mistaken. So if I went on seeing her for so long, if I cultivated our friendship attentively, it was also not to lose the knowledge of pain, so dearly bought. The last time, seven years ago, was during one of her trips to London. We arranged to meet at a tearoom like the two old ladies we had become, which I found rather amusing, when you think of the arrogance of our youth, when Anna caused heads to turn as she walked through the exhibition rooms, whereas I thought only of my work, and then again of my work, as we stood on her candlelit rooftop merrily emptying huge glasses of French wine. She was still very beautiful, in fact—though she'd lost a great deal of weight fighting colon cancer, and the relapse would eventually kill her, two years later, but she was like a high priestess in her dove-colored cashmere shawl, with her hair cut short, dyed auburn. We ordered coffee, and of course after we exchanged our news about our respective lives—my research at the library and the holiday home Anna was having built in Perth—we eventually spoke about you, the way we always did whenever we met, although she hadn't seen you in four decades and, at the time, I hadn't for fifteen years. That day, describing your relationship, Anna had said, *It wasn't based on feelings, it was physical*—and there was pride in her voice, a wrenching pride coming from the diminished woman she had become, as if to remind the world that she had once had a body, and what a body. I would have liked to say, *I remember. I remember everything. I remember exactly what you were like as a young woman; I remember Frank, and I sometimes get the impression that all my energy goes into remembering, I remember so well, my memory is saturated with images and voices.* One day, I'd heard someone ask you what your wife looked like like, and you answered that you just happened to have a picture of her in your wallet, and afterwards I watched you take a rectangle of paper roughly four inches by five from an inner pocket, and unfold it and unfold it and unfold it before the man's flabbergasted gaze, he didn't even dare move, now, until you'd unfolded the entire print, or rather poster, of Annelieke—a full-length Annelieke, naked. You held it gracefully from the upper edge between two fingers, your arm raised, and it was almost as if she were there. *There you are, she's more or less like this, Anna*, you said, unperturbed.

"Yes," said Anna pensively when I had finished telling her my story. "Yes, I was more or less like that, it's true. And you see: it's not as if it changed anything."

In the spring of 1971, one afternoon Annelieke summoned me to her place. Given her tone of voice on the telephone, I knew instantly that something serious had happened. No sooner did I cross the threshold to your apartment than Anna said:

"Who is he sleeping with?"

"With you," I replied, terrified.

"Give over," she said sharply, raising one hand as if to strike me. "Answer my question, Helen. Who is he sleeping with?"

"With you," I said again, unable to come up with another name.

"Don't you get tired of protecting him all the time? I know about the studio, actually. The two of you really took me for a fool. And you didn't notice! For Christ's sake, Helen, what were you thinking? No big deal, maybe? Come and see! Just come and see!"

She dragged me roughly by the arm down the corridor to your pretend studio, a room I had only rarely seen before. She pulled a painting out from behind a piece of furniture and shouted, "Look at this picture! Who is this woman? It's not you, and it certainly isn't me."

So I looked closely at the picture. I had never seen her, of that I was sure. It was the portrait of a woman sitting in an armchair by a window through which one could literally smell the downpour and the odor of the leaves from the dripping trees. The woman was wearing a yellow jumper over blue

trousers, flat shoes, and a garnet scarf in her hair. She was looking straight at us, Anna and me, with no other expression than
her openness. And yet her face was blurred, the way Manet's
peonies in his still life with pruning shears are blurred, yet the
viewer knows unhesitatingly that they are peonies, even though
it is impossible to make out any details. The object is obviously
a peony, even though we can't really justify why that is, and in
your picture, there was something threatening us, even though
we were incapable of saying why we had this painful intuition.
In her impassivity, the woman was addressing us, informing us
of her arrival, but neither stepping closer to the canvas nor
moving back enabled us to determine who she was. She was
neither Anna nor me, on that score Anna had been right, with
her woman-in-love possessiveness. The subject of the painting
was much shorter than Anna was, that much was clear at first
glance, and she didn't look like me, either—you would never
have painted me in that position, never portrayed me not doing
something, and it was this, more than the woman's features,
which convinced me I was looking at a picture of someone
else. But who? The production of the painting was more classic than what you had habitually done thus far, and the change
of style seemed to announce a change of season, the end of one
cycle and the beginning of another. Nor was she an imaginary
woman. She was a woman who existed somewhere, even if we
had never seen her, and you were sharing feelings with her,
feelings we had not known you possessed in your emotional
range. I could not bring myself to look away, I examined each
detail one by one as if they could tell me her secret. I felt as if
I'd opened a door onto someone's private life, as if I were spy-
ing on something that did not belong to me, that had nothing
to do with me. On second thought, I did suppose that you had
known we would find the portrait, sooner or later—otherwise
why would you have stored the canvas here, in your pretend-
studio, your gallery-studio where Annelieke spent almost more

time than you did, and not at the clandestine studio on Prinsenstraat, which you knew I occasionally went up to, out of curiosity, though I had not crossed the threshold since the day I had read your poem, as if the room were equipped with some museum alarm system against intruders. I would never have found the canvas if you had stored it at our place as you had here, behind a piece of furniture—but Annelieke did find it, just as you had known she would. Why, then? I did not share my thoughts with you, however, and so I don't know whether you were even aware of the issue, or whether, engrossed in your dilemma, rather, your response was to resort instinctively to this ploy, in order to inform us of what was lurking in the murky depths of your heart. I have never forgotten that picture. Even today, I can almost capture the smell of varnish and turpentine in the room where I stood that day next to Anna, unable to do anything at all to reassure her.

The woman in the painting was called Margo. She had only just turned eighteen, she manufactured lamps while studying art, and for a few months you'd been crazy about her until she ditched you ruthlessly for her ethnology professor, a bald man thirty years her senior. When she left, you even categorically refused to return the belongings she'd left at Prinsenstraat, declaring with your usual arrogance that she'd be back so it was pointless to move them for nothing, but she didn't come back. She married her professor and gave him four children by the time she was thirty. You were flattered, I suppose, to have been able to seduce such a young girl, but then to see yourself discarded for someone who at the time seemed like an old man to us was an unspeakable affront. This stormy relationship did, however, bring about the end of your life with Anna, and the beginning of another life—more unstable, more catatonic, where one girl followed another in your bed. With your relationship with Anna behind you, you officially moved back to Prinsenstraat. The pictures you painted, the honors you received, the money you earned— what can I tell you that you don't already know? It would be an incredible story to tell, and to be honest, I think I've always imagined that one day I would write a book about your career—that after spending my life only a few yards away from you writing so many books on so many other subjects, I would one day end up producing something about your work, to tell the world what I, your best friend, had seen. But in the end, I did not write your story, as I have just realized. I thought I had, though; I even certainly, sincerely thought at times that I had. Sometimes we think about a project so intensely that it seems we have actually gone through with it, when in fact we've done no such thing. There is something of you, of course, in all my books, but I never wrote directly about you—perhaps because the thought of reducing you to a book seemed unworthy of you. It is amazing when I happen, out of the blue, to come upon one of the paintings you produced during our life together. I might see it on television, in an art magazine or, of course, at a museum, solidly fastened to the wall and protected by a placid guard and an alarm, and I'll remember the circumstances behind the canvas's creation, the different stages, a canvas I saw in our home, or lying on the floor at the studio, or emerging before my eyes from some glittery gift wrapping at Christmas, now hanging in a public space surrounded by a multitude of warnings. Each time, entire scenes come back to me, flashbacks that have no mutual connection other than the vision of the painting in the background. I saw those paintings, but they saw me, too. If they could speak, they would tell my entire story.

Yes, if they could speak, I am sure your paintings would betray me. They would tell of my stupidity, my blindness, my dishonesty, and my selfishness. They would say how, because I had failed to seduce you, I now took pride in the fact you had come back to live near me, and seemed openly dependent on the all the good things I did for you. I was certainly not the most beautiful, nor the most gifted of the women around you, but I was, apparently, the only one you needed, the only one who had never been replaced by anyone else, the one who did not have to beg for your presence over the phone the way assorted female voices did every week. All I had to do was go lightly up the steps to the top floor of my own house and knock on the door. It was as if I were hiding an alluring fugitive, or holding prisoner the coveted princess from a fairy tale. In public you would put your arm warmly around my shoulders, and declare to anyone who would listen, *Do you know Helen? I could not manage without her!* And I was absurdly flattered by your words, so much so as to forget their burdensome subtext—the daily upkeep, the organization, the sheer *labor* it took to look after everything for you. I would give a modest smile and tell the people there with us, *He's had too much to drink, don't believe a word,* then I took the glass from your hand, so that you would be fit to work the next day. I had become your servant, and like all servants, I had ended up presuming that my master belonged to me.

B ut we did great things in those years, from 1971 to 1975. In the apartment on Prinsenstraat, we got up early and went to bed late. We had ideal reserves of energy in those days—no doubt I am burnishing my memories, like some dull metal that turns to gold the more you rub it—but all I remember are sunny mornings walking in the salty little Amsterdam breeze, and a healthy diet, plenty to drink, and the work coming in, miraculously. I had at last seriously begun work on the book about Thomas Hardy I'd been wanting to write for so long, and which for years I seemed to have been getting nowhere with. Now the words came as if by magic: at five o'clock in the morning I was already at work, pounding feverishly on the keyboard of my typewriter, my eyes riveted to the paper. Spread across the desk were various volumes of Hardy's work, which I had previously annotated in vain, unable to produce anything coherent from them—and now they seemed to be whispering their story to me, without restraint. Day after day, word by word, they dictated the book I was meant to write. The pile of pages grew, and when I reread my work in the evening, I was stunned by what I had managed to do. In this book, I passionately defended a bold theory that Hardy's use of dialogue was basically very similar to that of the plays by the eighteenth-century Italian playwright Carlo Goldoni: on first reading, the lines seem to follow one after the other in a sort of chaotic unfurling, and then the rhythm accelerates and all at once the entire exchange makes sense, and it's enough to break your heart, the way everything is perfectly structured. As a rule, there is a group of villagers who play the role of a Greek chorus, enhancing the main action with their commentary. Initially it seemed that Hardy wrote these dialogues very much as they came to him, carried by his own inspiration, but in fact everything was beautiful, and carefully thought through. No one reads Hardy much these days, or so I've heard. The first time I read him it was because I'd heard that F. Scott Fitzgerald said that the millionaires in his stories were "as beautiful and damned as Thomas Hardy's peasants." Fitzgerald is viewed now as a drunkard, but that, alas, does not do justice to the soundness of his literary judgment, and I believe that on that score, at any rate, he was right. In *Far from the Madding Crowd* there is an episode where the poor shepherd Gabriel Oak is trying to find out what he needs to know to ask for young Bathsheba's hand in marriage, and from his aunt he learns that he will not be the first to ask for it. His immediate, unfortunate resolution is among the most tragic lines in Western literature. *"That's unfortunate," said Farmer Oak, contemplating a crack in the stone floor with sorrow. "I'm only an every-day sort of man, and my only chance was in being the first comer . . ."* It is only recently, on coming across this book in my library by chance, a book written nearly a hundred and fifty years ago, that I have been able to grasp its hidden meaning. I, Helen, was well and truly the first comer in your life, and yet, like Gabriel Oak, I was destined to wander for years before the object of my love could see me. Do you see me now? Frank, my books—all my books—are about nothing but you.

A nd so, after an interval of four years, you had come back, and nothing seemed to have changed—but in fact, everything had changed. For years I had been the youngest wherever I went, but from that point on your mistresses began to dethrone me. There were dozens of them, young women splattered with bright paint, accosted as they left art school, ambitious and ethereal, and I would find them in my kitchen early in the morning, trying to tame my coffee maker. In those years you began painting portraits, just as if you were adding a new string to your bow. It was a way for you to get girls, too, to go on seducing them, as you headed reluctantly towards middle age. Now I can tell you: there was something a bit pathetic about the way you used to go up to them in cafés and offer to paint them, and the way you would introduce yourself, and smile. Once you were famous, the girls sometimes recognized you: they probably wouldn't have done so *everywhere*, but in Amsterdam, by the early 1970s, you had acquired a certain local glory, and so, the whole lot of them eagerly accepted your request. Many of them informed you at the first session at your studio that they had left their waitressing job in order to be available for the sittings, and what that really meant was, *available for you, Frank Appledore,* because your reputation as a lover preceded you. And then the girls must have heard about those love-radiant portraits you had painted of Anna or Margo, and so, when you offered to paint them, the subtext of what they heard was surely something like, *Come with me and I'll make you a queen, a muse, the way I have with the other women I loved;* but you were no longer the Frank who knew how to do that with a woman. You no longer wanted to make a lasting commitment. You were perfectly glad to have resumed our former cohabitation, you relied on my faithful presence precisely not to have to go looking for a woman for any length of time beyond a few nights. You painted, and I took care of our domestic life—as for the rest, for all you knew you were twenty years old again. Years later, during one of my tête-à-têtes with Anna, when we were once again scrutinizing your conduct, in particular regarding that sudden reversal of behavior, she told me the story of how Matisse, when ordered by his legitimate wife to choose between her and his mistress, asked her to let him think it over for two days and eventually replied that he would rather keep his mistress, because she was the only one who could help him fill out his tax returns. We had both turned thirty-three that year, and these would be our last four years of shared life for a long while. We were no longer altogether young, and the fact we were still living together at that age, still living according to a certain rhythm we'd grown accustomed to, began to weigh with significance. Some faces had vanished from our circle, here and there, alliances had formed, couplings had yielded to families—people were growing up, in a way, whereas the two of us were still in the eye of the hurricane, where things happened. You didn't seem to give it any thought, but I did, often. We were changing, and the portraits were also a sign of that change.

That year my father died of a heart attack, without warning, on the marble floor in the entryway of the house in Rhodes where he had been living with my mother. My brothers came to the funeral with their respective spouses—whom I'd never seen other than at their weddings and on the family photographs they sent me (although God knows why) during the holiday season—and that day, as we stood around our mother to support her, they looked me scornfully up and down from the height of their marital status because I was alone. I was only thirty-three, after all, and I had just lost my father; it hadn't occurred to me to look for an escort. Even a companion would have seemed too showy an adornment under the circumstances. I had not told any of my friends that my father had died. As for you, I'd forbidden you from coming, and although you protested, you eventually relented. I wished I could have been alone by the coffin, to be able to think about what had happened, or at least only with my mother and brothers, just the five of us the way we used to be back in the days when we were a family. I would have liked simply to sit out in the grass, there by the opening ready to receive his coffin, and think, in my laborious way, think about him and the life we had had together, the father he had been, the daughter I had been, rather than shaking a hundred hands, standing next to my brothers who wanted to humiliate me because I wasn't married. Our father had meant much more to me than he had to them, and so I think I also missed him more. For all his faults, his sudden loss left me feeling terribly disorientated, because I had built myself *against* him, and building oneself against someone also means leaning on them, and in the months that followed his death my clearest sensation was one of a loss of balance. I went back to Amsterdam feeling quite wretched, in that house where you and I lived, full of laughter and people, of books and paintings, but devoid of anyone who truly loved me. Devoid of a great love, devoid of a comprehensible future. Of whatever it was my father had hoped for me. He had always looked down on you, and while I don't think our cohabitation broke his heart, he certainly did not view it kindly. I came home feeling very lost, transformed, confused. As for my brothers, the last time I saw them, scarcely ten years later at my mother's funeral, the wives had vanished from the scene. Fred stank of alcohol, and Maarten couldn't stop nervously wrinkling his nose and regularly going back and forth to the toilets at the crematorium, making very little effort to be discreet. When his turn came to speak from the rostrum, he mumbled a few inaudible words, while we all watched, dumbfounded, as a line of bright red blood trickled from one of his nostrils. The sensation must eventually have bothered him, because he suddenly wiped his nose with the back of his hand, several times, and finished singing our mother's praises with his face streaked in blood. Fred, next to me, had already been peacefully snoring for several minutes. And yet, in the years that followed, to my great astonishment, I again received New Year's greetings—cards that were, how to put it, more chaotic; one or the other of my brothers with a woman whose face seemed to change every year, either because it actually was a new woman, or because cosmetic surgery had something to do with it, and the children, all the children, growing indiscriminately obese and vacuous beneath a luxurious Christmas tree. Now when I walk past a fiftysomething tramp in the street, beaming with stupidity and reeking of filth, I instantly wonder whether it mightn't be one of my nephews.

My family did remind me of its presence, over the years, but there was also your family. Your mother was still in Paimpol, and even though you nurtured a steely grudge against her, in your way you loved her passionately, and so you painted horses and self-portraits for her, always one or the other. You would send them to her two at a time—one painting of horses, one of yourself, bubble-wrapped face to face. Your self-portraits were striking, but the horses were more interesting. Your creatures were not Wouwerman's warhorses, although he certainly inspired you. No, you painted wild horses, alone on the plain, horses that belonged to no one. And when you got angry with Kate, for a change, you would send her dead horses. It was a veritable anthology: during one of your fallings out, you read everything you could on the subject, and Malaparte's anecdote about the horses of Lake Ladoga in particular. That story inspired an entire series of deformed horses' heads emerging from the ice, and you never tired of explaining to all our friends the phenomenon of supercooling, which was at the origin of the tragedy: under normal conditions, water turns solid when the temperature drops below zero degrees, but if the chill is extremely rapid and the water is perfectly pure, ice cannot form without the presence of the germs that allow the crystals to develop. Malaparte's horses, therefore, had in all probability upset the precarious balance of supercooling by displacing masses of water and introducing their own impurities—blades of grass, earth, hair—and thus had unwittingly hastened their own fate. You loved that story, your mother far less so. She rang me after she'd received the package and asked to speak to you, but seemed quite pleased to hear you'd gone out, and so asked me, instead: *Do you know what I could possibly have done to him, Helen, for him to go sending me those ghastly things?* I was speechless. You were literally drowning her with your horses, at one point in time, as if you'd figured out that your art could also be a weapon, a way of taking revenge on your family—but of course that, too, eventually backfired on you. Whenever we went to see Kate together, once or twice a year, you would carefully count the number of paintings that hung all the way up to the chandeliers—and there were systematically more pictures of horses than there were portraits of you. When you pointed this out to her, Kate shrugged and said:

"But in some of them you look so much like your father, I cannot have them hanging in my house. I haven't come this far just to keep looking at your father's face. Horses, at least, don't remind me of anyone."

"But the pictures *go together*, Mother. They are diptychs. You cannot do this."

"The very idea! A portrait of you with one of a horse. Besides, you hate horses. Enough of your nonsense."

And Kate went off to give instructions to her cook, while you clambered up onto the furniture to remove the paintings and re-arrange them as you saw fit. You went all the way up to the attic—*The bitch, I know they're up here*—to find the pictures she had rejected, and pounded whatever nails you could find into the frames to make them hold. When Kate came back, she did not even raise her eyes before she said:

"You will put everything back as it was before leaving, Frankie."

Which you did, every time, sick at heart, there before her powdered eyes, while with a knowing look she offered me an after-dinner almond brandy. Afterwards, she kissed you on the forehead, and we set off in your Chrysler, driving through the night back to Amsterdam, and when you lifted one hand to adjust your glasses I could clearly see the deep imprint your fingers had left in the leather on the steering wheel, from squeezing it so hard.

Y ou were nervous because you were worried. That year, I know, you had watched with despair as Ossip's career suddenly took off. You were torn between your affection for this man who was one of your best friends, and your burning desire to assert publicly that his work, in your opinion, was completely overrated. Ever since your early success you'd thought you were indisputably at the head of the pack, and now suddenly you were being overtaken. The slightest little piece of news you had to share—a sale, an offer for an exhibition, an article—was instantly supplanted by news of Ossip. Dear old Ossip was not at fault, and there was even, at least so I thought, a sort of loyalty in the way he didn't hide anything from you or try to deceive you with silence, and you knew it, but that did not change the fact that you found the situation atrociously painful. You were beginning to dread running into him, and were probably also counting the days until things would go back to normal and your own triumph would prevail. Everything you had wanted for yourself was now happening in someone else's life. This gave you a feeling of shame, as if a package addressed to you had been delivered by mistake to a neighbor across the landing and you had mysteriously failed to recover your property, although you knew full well that this vision of events was a sin of jealousy. Only to me did you dare to say, late at night, tense with frustration, brandishing a glass of water and a cigarette:

"Of course it sells. He paints portraits of Nazis, after all. And anyway, what the fuck do we care, we're artists, not philosophers."

In a way, you were right. Ossip claimed he was useless at business, but the truth was that with his gap-toothed simpleton's face and his clever brain he worked wonders, because no one suspected him. He aroused a sort of pity in people which always worked to his advantage. The art world was completely besotted with his emotional expressiveness, his naïve colors, his evasive pronouncements. He produced rough portraits of Heydrich, Goebbels, Goering, and Himmler in domestic scenes, with no explanation of his process, whereas your incredible horses were seen as an anachronistic passion. But it was true, too, that you had never made up for the lost time of your late start—whenever anyone mentioned a young artist in your presence, your face grew tense with pain. You couldn't forgive yourself for having missed your chance at being a precocious genius, for not having found your vocation until you were twenty-eight. You were intensely jealous of all the young painters you met, including those who were patently less talented than you— and I believe you were terribly ashamed of your jealousy. You had exasperating faults, but you were not cruel. You were not beyond lying, however, in certain situations—but we're all liars in the end: the moment we apply words to our experience, we opt for a certain version of things, to the detriment of any other possible version; every word in itself contains an interpretation, and beyond the words even the order in which we describe events can considerably alter the impact of our story—obviously, the sequence we describe always belies our reading of the facts, the place where we want to situate ourselves, all the underlying emotions we might be feeling without realizing it. It's a cliché to point this out, but when someone's ideas become public, as yours very quickly did, these inevitable constructions are suddenly given an uncontrollable range, becoming the stuff of legend, and little by little a story takes shape and comes to replace any other utterances, any competing reality. You had always been eloquent, loquacious, a smooth talker, but under the effect of your ever more constant presence in the media you wasted no time in grasping the power of communication, the importance of impacting people's minds and infinitely expanding your control over what might be said about you. You knew the value of silence, the science of leaving voids in your autobiography, voids where others could fantasize—to your advantage—about your secret exploits, without you ever having to put them right, as you were not the one who had come up with them. Thus the whispered legend spread that you had been painting since childhood, that somewhere on the planet there were pictures and drawings that were proof of your virtuosity, although no one had ever found them—for good reason. You allowed the doubt to remain, like some golden rain that would inevitably grace your forehead, because the only person who could contradict you was me.

Over the years you changed, of course. Success changed you, but deep down very little—what happened was that another version of your self progressively took shape alongside reality, almost like a hologram, a public Frank Appledore, about whom articles and catalogues were written, and subsequently, books and dissertations and monographs, and while that Frank was not a complete stranger to me he was nevertheless a separate incarnation of the person I knew and had grown up with, and now lived with. It was both extremely strange and of no importance whatsoever. Whether we are famous or not, our reputation always precedes us, all of us, and the fact that yours was particularly brilliant and full of ups and downs mattered little to our shared life. Sometimes photographers would show up on the doorstep with a mission from an art magazine to do a feature on you, and I would watch them picking out accessories, installing you in front of your own canvases and even, quite often, asking you not to wash your paint-splattered forearms, so that the image would look more authentic. *Artist Frank Appledore in his studio.* The pictures were magnificent, but I sometimes thought that to portray you as you really were, they should have preserved for posterity your unlaced leather shoes abandoned at the foot of the stairs, your nail clippings by the sink, the three packs of cigarettes you placed almost solemnly on the windowsill when you came into the kitchen in the morning, and my little self, always in the background, always. That was who you were, Frank. Because I was the one who was working so hard to keep our entire life going.

D id you never wonder why I got married, in the spring of 1975? That wasn't like me, was it, to go and get married on a whim. Did you really never ask yourself why? The simplest explanation, I now realize, could be summed up as follows: *It was a drastic measure, but I hadn't expected you to not try and stop me.* More subtly, I'm forced to admit that my love life had been a failure. I'd had lovers, but the unpleasantness I'd experienced with the first one, Erik, had never left me. I'd learned a lot, during the first half of my life; I'd really grown up, I'd been so happy, but I never felt close to the men I went out with. They left me feeling deeply disappointed, every one. Some lacked energy, others kindness, others any sort of literary culture—whatever the case, sooner or later, irremediably, I would end up going home in the middle of the night to find you sitting there scribbling in the kitchen, and we would finish the night together talking and laughing. I wondered why no one had ever said to me the extraordinary things I heard in songs (you probably never wondered, either, why for six long tiresome months I went out with that young folk guitarist with the pony tail who didn't get your jokes—well, now you know). I was also to blame, to be sure. I never felt fully present, I was like those people who are careful always to sleep with one leg or foot sticking out from under the covers, to feel the cool outside air. In a way, your old poem was telling the truth—I had never been in love, except with you, certainly, but that was so long ago, and I thought that it had evolved into something else since then. I loved the solitude of my study, but I was beginning to panic at the thought that I was already thirty-seven years old and didn't have any success to speak of in my love life. You had become an artist against all expectations—now I wanted to do something incredible, too.

That was why, in part, when Günther Merens, a forty-three-year-old architect, proposed to me on our fourth meeting, I immediately accepted. We were in a French restaurant in the antiques quarter, and he proposed while we were waiting for dessert. He did not hide the engagement ring in my food because, as he later explained, he thought that would be ridiculous and he knew I shared his opinion. But I wasn't sure I found it all that ridiculous, actually. Later I would sometimes recall that detail and conclude that right from the start there had been a misunderstanding between us, in the way Günther had of overestimating our affinities or my compliance with his expectations, but at the time, it is true that I was charmed by the way he claimed to know what I liked, by his deep respect for my intellectual qualities, and by his proposal, which was so sober and dignified. No one had ever treated me like that, regarded me in that way. Spending so much time around you had meant my affairs were mainly with artists or art students—cultured, snobbish, unpredictable, and in no time I began to appear rigid to them—after the initial pleasure of drinking wine and eating shrimp and coconut milk soup in cheap Vietnamese restaurants, I had to return to work and stick to my schedule—hardly compatible with the perpetual fiesta that seemed to make up their daily lives. These arrogant young lovers found my serious nature depressing; I, in exchange, felt oppressed by their light-heartedness. Günther, however, would drive me to Haarlem on weekends to show me around building sites, and I appreciated his rigor, his bright eyes, the spots of faded green ink on the back of his square hands with their neatly-trimmed nails, his habit of picking up a brick here and there on the building sites, or thrusting his whole fist into a sandbag, or tapping a slab of marble with an expert phalanx to test its quality. I liked his punctuality, his calm manner, his indisputably *adult* behavior, so much so that I could not picture him as a child, as if one day he had suddenly burst from the earth in this finished form, with his chest hairs and silver cuff links. All my life I had been wary of adults, but now for the first time here was one whom I desired with all my heart. I think I loved the image of myself that Günther reflected back to me, that of an educated, reasonable woman, circumspect, cool-headed and full of common sense. I had just turned thirty-seven, my professional life was as ideal as my love life was disastrous, and so I desperately wanted to be that woman he described to me. Perhaps, too, far more simply, I wanted someone to love me.

With hindsight, I can see that I probably chose Günther because he had nothing in common with you. He was a businessman, not a showman; a technician, not an artist. He was earnest, reliable, serious. He was prickly, where you were proud. Günther did not have a sense of humor—something I probably took in the beginning as a proof of depth. He was not dazzling, he never relaxed except in places earmarked for leisure—hotels, bars, cruises—and he always ate in a hurry, from the corner of a table, never looking at his plate, jabbing his fork while his eyes were glued to a blueprint or a model. He did not know how to dance, but he could drive the most complicated, overequipped cars with a rare ease, cars in which I could hardly find the ignition and was completely disoriented by the profusion of knobs and buttons. He was intensely masculine—stocky, hairy, always in a suit, with polished leather shoes, a supply of paper clips, a stapler, and a pair of Eames lounge chairs. His father had been a carpenter, and he had worked with him on building sites to pay for his architecture studies. He had no one to thank for his money but himself; he regularly inspected his invoices and his bank statements, yet was offended if I wanted to pay for something out of my own pocket. He wanted children, a dog, a house in the country or on the coast; his only male acquaintances were men just like him; he vaguely avoided their wives and fiancées, and did not have any close female friends, with the exception, perhaps, of the few he had gone out with before we were married, each of whom he took out to dinner once a year to an extravagant restaurant in order to swap news. He worshipped his mother, hated music, and saw the space around him solely in the form of lines. Colors, textures, and elements of style were completely lost on him. On the rare occasion when I was able to drag him to a museum or gallery opening, he would pace through the rooms with a heavy stride, his fists rammed into his pockets, and out of the corner of my eye I would see him stop in front of a painting, bring his face closer to the surface, step back, shake his head, and set off again. Even the hors d'oeuvres laid out for guests at these events seemed to annoy him, their small size unsuitable for his fingers. To have lived so long with you then choose a man like this, was bound to mean something: it was as if I were implicitly manifesting my curiosity or my weariness, or my desire to make a life for myself, one from which you would, de facto, be excluded.

You didn't see it coming. In an incredibly short time I'd fallen in love and become a fiancée. For the first time in my life, or very nearly, I was tied to someone more solidly than I was to you. Günther had literally supplanted you. I no longer came to knock at your studio door at the end of the day to suggest a glass of wine—I was out with the man I loved, and it was with him that I was drinking, otherwise, if I was at home, now you were the one who came and knocked at my door in vain, because I was busy making love, making love with this new man who had come into my life, this man who was slightly older than we were, who was consistent and respectable, and whose vigorous thrusts caused the springs of my mother's hand-carved bed to creak. Günther clashed with the décor of our Amsterdam apartment, as if he were too modern. He had trouble squeezing through its narrow recesses, he would bump into paintings, and one day he broke a fragile Directoire stool I'd inherited from my grandmother, simply by bursting out laughing. But I loved him all day and all night. I would nestle into his pale shoulders, let him break whatever he liked, on condition that he would repair me. After lovemaking, he sometimes fell asleep like a log, a very beautiful and dignified sleep, very pictorial—Günther had the heavy, charming face of a peasant by Brueghel the Younger, leaning on his sack of wheat, pipe in hand, his thick canvas smock wrinkled and open at the neck. There were other times, however, when he did not sleep at all, and lay alert and restless in the bed, enormous, naked, his legs spread wide across the sheet, revealing his heavy, resting penis, until he would reach for a shirt and a pair of trousers to go down to the kitchen for a snack, then come back up with a plate of sweet pickles in one hand and a hunk of bread and cheese in the other, a bottle of claret tucked under his arm and his fingers curled around two crystal glasses. It was so—so *different*. One floor above, you were furiously at work in your studio with its fug of chemical smells, and it all seemed like a world I had irretrievably left behind, Alice slipping down the rabbit-hole on her way to new adventures. I no longer went up to the fourth floor, I went and shut myself in my study to work until Günther came to fetch me, at lunch or dinner-time, and then we spent our nights in a relentless embrace, his massive body and my tiny little one. I had never been so self-centered. I no longer bothered to check whether there was anything in the fridge, or whether the cleaning woman had come by. I had nothing at all to do with the upkeep of this space I'd been sharing with my best friend for almost twenty years—no. I devoted myself to my relationship; I bought clothes, let my hair grow, luxuriated in the pleasure of being treated like a woman in love. Normally so cautious and solitary, under the charm of my new affair I had let down all my barriers. That is probably why I only found out *after* I had married Günther Merens that unbeknownst to me, my decision implied another one: I would go with him when he moved to Boston, Massachusetts, where he had just obtained a position with an up-and-coming architectural firm.

Had my fiancé deliberately arranged for this information not to reach my ears until it was too late? I never found out, but indisputably the result looked for all the world like an underhanded kidnapping strategy. At the time, however, I swore that I was pleased with the way things were going: my life was about to be completely turned on its ear, and I could ask for nothing better. Not only had I found love, but I was going with my lover to a foreign country, and it was like a honeymoon made specifically for us, because it would be both realistic and prolonged. If I had been more honest, though, I would surely have vented my anger, or astonishment, at having so readily accepted my imprisonment. I would have defended my position, asserted my right not to leave my circle of friends or abandon my professional network. I would have invoked my unbearable childhood, being carted about at the mercy of my father's postings, I would have insisted that I wouldn't put up with it anymore, I would have maintained that I had earned the privilege once and for all not to ever have to move again against my will, that I had the right to choose where I wanted to live without anyone deciding for me. It took me years, in fact, to dare to say how hurt I was by Günther's unilateral decision, and like in the fairy tale, where a simple pea hidden under twenty mattresses was enough to torment the rain-drenched young girl who shows up in the kingdom, claiming to be of royal origin, this tiny detail which surfaced in the early days of my marriage to Günther never ceased to feel like a painful pea in our bed. It tormented both of us and led us towards an ending far less glorious than the one in Andersen's fairy tale.

I went ahead and packed my suitcases like a good girl, tidied the house, held a farewell party. Gave a joyful kiss to everyone I was fond of, as if leaving them behind was not actually a painful experience. On the plane I read frenetically, the first volume of *The Americans* by Library of Congress director Daniel Boorstin, and I looked out the window at the stars and the surface of the Atlantic Ocean, while Günther incomprehensibly fell fast asleep on my shoulder. *The colonies*, wrote Boorstin with his usual precision, *were a disproving ground for utopias.*

N ow I can hardly remember the years I spent in Boston, as if another person had lived through them and told me the story afterwards, and I'd only half listened. Occasionally I will recall certain phrases I would repeat over and over at the time, whenever one of our Boston acquaintances asked how I felt about the city and life in America. I do not know what is true. I seem to recall that I liked the city, its venerable dignity, its open-mindedness, its night life, its past as the American capital of the press, its blizzards, and its humid, continental climate, typical of New England. In the early years, Günther and I would go on long walks where he guided me through the city and described the long succession of architectural styles—Paul Revere's house with its diamond-shaped glass windows, the Georgian facades on Washington Street with their characteristic windows, Quincy Market with its Doric columns, the Italianate style of the Athenaeum, the neighborhoods of South End and Back Bay, built in the late nineteenth century under the esthetic influence of the Parisian *grands boulevards* ordained by Napoléon III, Trinity Church, the Grain Exchange, or the Gothic Cummings and Sears buildings, inspired by John Ruskin's theories; but also the fantastical, extraordinary buildings on Mount Vernon Street, with their sunflower motifs, and a few colonial-style edifices, the gray granite, the grandiose arrogance of South Station, the Art Deco style of the old shoe factory, the glass modernism imported by European architects who'd fled the Nazis.

Günther was a good talker, and I will always be grateful to him for the hours he spent presenting Boston to me on a platter of words, with his precision and technical lyricism. He made the city come alive for me—this town founded by fleeing English puritans—and now it was my city, too, whether I wanted it to be or not. We had a roomy apartment on Beacon Hill, and I was working a great deal. I quickly established professional connections locally, and was working as a freelance scout for two American publishing houses; I was translating, now and again, I put people in touch across the pond, I felt useful. But—and perhaps it had nothing to do with the long walks we took, governed by Günther's love affair with stone—I also felt myself becoming somewhat rigid, too stable, almost mineral, I found it hard to breathe. When I spoke about it with my husband, he replied with a smile that I was probably just taking my first hesitant steps in the real world, after spending so many years in the whirlwind of my youth with you, a youth which, in his opinion, had lasted a bit longer than necessary, and now it was time for me to adapt. And I was indeed adapting, but it was rather terrifying. Why hide it: I missed you so much. I have nothing left to hide. When I left you, I lost all my bearings. For years on end I had been used to being immersed in work, because I knew that all I ever had to do was open the door to your room and I could see you and laugh with you about anything, and take a break, in our house that was always full, with people always dropping by. Now I was alone all day long, at home or in the office I rented in Back Bay. Günther came home at night with a bottle of French wine, and we had dinner just the two of us in the kitchen on the marble island, perched on uncomfortable stools. I didn't even dare venture to tell him, but I greatly missed my old wood-paneled apartment with its baroque space and creaking doors. I liked the strangeness of my new life, which I even qualified as *exotic* in the beginning, when I would congratulate myself for having left, for having made a move, at the age of thirty-seven, for having taken a risk on a new country, but deep down I mourned constantly for my European homeland, with its narrow, winding streets, irregular paving stones, and cozy familiarity, so small you could put your arms around it. It was *a bit too big* in America, that's what I would have liked to tell Günther—but that was probably the one phrase above all others that an architect could not stand hearing.

S till, after the terrifying first weeks, I regained my energy, or rather, my survival instincts replenished my energy. I worked a tremendous amount during those years. In all likelihood, my professional success enabled to me to ignore my personal malaise. I sometimes told myself that, quite simply, as Günther would say, I was forty years old now, and not thirty, and the slightly bitter taste to life now was one of maturity, sobriety, gravity. When our new acquaintances urged me to tell them about my life in Europe I did what they asked, and smiled indulgently at my own escapades; I claimed to be glad such things were now well and truly behind me. Of course, under my husband's satisfied gaze I lied diligently: it had all been very amusing and very hectic, but nowadays I could not possibly survive on so little sleep, or live in such chaos. I was glad to have such a solid, sensible life now—and besides, who would want to stay forever in the blindness and stupidity of youth? Did we not all agree that we knew ourselves better now, that our lost illusions had educated and shaped us, incommensurably, and for nothing on earth would we want to return to the completely overrated doldrums of our twenties? Wasn't it wonderful to feel serene at last, and powerful, and free—freer, in fact, than ever before? When the weather was fine we went to Revere Beach, said to be the oldest public beach in the United States, so we learned, and while Günther fell asleep with his nose in a book about Walter Gropius, I found myself staring obsessively at the horizon, towards Europe.

N aturally, *to flee* does not only mean to leave a place, but also to head towards a new one. I did not agree to marry Günther Merens because he was offering me a desirable way out, but because I loved him. I loved his pragmatism, the way he took himself seriously, his dexterity, his business savvy, his graph paper, his authority, and his knowledge. I liked walking with him and listening to him describing the buildings around us, I liked his silences too, his regularity— you were like a firework, and watching fireworks for too long eventually becomes tiring, whereas Günther resonated dully like a quality boiler, a more modest device, but noble, more reliable, with a mechanical hum that has something comforting about it. After spending years reassuring you, providing a framework for you, I suppose I wanted to find myself in an arrangement that would allow me to play the opposite role, to be the one who had everything taken care of for her, the one for whom time and space were cleared—I wanted to be the most important thing in someone's life and Günther, undeniably, gave me that, with that marvelous way he had of being nothing but certainty. Günther solved problems; you created them, caused them, made them worse. I was working more and more, things were going well, and I wanted a partner who would respect my activities and my skills, and not make fun of them. With Günther, I could work in peace; he had the greatest respect for work, and he did not distinguish between its various incarnations, nor did he feel threatened by my legitimate desire to have a career. Only years later, once we had lost touch with each other at the very heart of our marriage, when our house was hissing with frustration and we could not touch without scraping each other, I reproached him for having wanted me as an asset, the literary wife he could show off to colleagues as proof of his refinement, his openness, because I knew that deep down he had been glad of the difference in our temperaments and occupations, pleased to be the only one in his circle of school friends who had not married an architect or project manager, who had taken a different path and married outside his comfort zone—even though I also knew that his diligence in criticizing those endogamous unions was a compliment addressed to me, his way of reminding me that he had no regrets. Like most people, once I started retreating from our love story, I initially placed the blame on my partner. I drew upon the memorable moments of our early days to fashion my weapons, hewn from the very matter of our understanding, and thus unparalleled in their efficacy to undo that understanding. I distorted his words as I changed sides, I provoked him, humiliated him, did everything I could to wring tears from him, I burned what I had loved, because when we are leaving someone, in the beginning we often try to say farewell to a version of ourselves that has come to seem too narrow, too time-worn, and we struggle violently to break free of it as if it were a poisoned shirt of Nessus.

There were times during those years, from 1975 to 1980, when at a dinner party or elsewhere, someone who was a bit more curious than the others asked me if I had any news of you—you were not yet as famous as you would later become, but all the same, a few people in our elite circle had heard of you, and followed your career with keener attention now that they were conscious of the fact that I knew you. These same people sometimes took me to one side to ask, with a disturbing blend of complicity and voyeurism, whether I *did not miss you a great deal*, and I would think, *a great deal? When we miss someone, it is always a great deal, isn't it?* But I was always slightly tipsy, back then, I think, so my answer was, No, we have got used to it, and in any case, we did write to each other, you and I, an abundance of letters. I did not tell them how I wept in the elevator. I did not say that your letters had no smell, no warmth, no muscles, that they arrived without warning in compact little bundles splattered with paint, and I avidly unwrapped them and read them over and over again the moment I could, but those rectangles of paper could not replace my best friend, could not make me forget your absence. I censored myself. That was all I did, all the time. I can see it now. I forbade myself, with a rigor that even I found excessive, from saying how much I regretted everything, how awkward and unsatisfied I felt with this new order of things. Innocently, Günther liked to share with his friends his first impressions of my apartment in Amsterdam, and he was

insanely eloquent in describing the *vie de bohème* he had res-
cued me from, according to his lights. Some of the wives pretended to be wiping tears of laughter from their eyes as they listened to him, while I smiled tactfully, playing my assigned role
of the woman-child. I pretended to go along with his story of
miraculous salvation, to believe in the candor I used to have, as
if, at the age of thirty-seven, I really could have been that childish girl he displayed in his memorama—but as the years went
by I could hear, ever more clearly, a rumbling inside me, like
some noise from an underground current which, as the soil
eroded—our love—progressively ended up submerging everything, until the day I stood in front of Günther screaming at
him that I had loved it all, that I knew what I was doing back
then, that I had thoroughly loved my apartment, all the time,
filled as it was to overflowing, and I had loved my shared life
with you, I hadn't missed a thing, that it had been my life, and
I would not have traded it for any other. That I was not *adrift*
when he met me, I was an independent woman who had real
friends and a career. I did not want him to speak of my apartment as if it were a battlefield, or of my old life as if it were a
mistake. And then I thought, *What about you, Günther? Who
were you when I met you? What made you so much better, in
the years before I came along? In those days, you were nothing
more than what you are now, an architect on a salary. Why
should my life at the time have been more dubious than the one
you were leading? What was less worthy about it? My house,
back then, was overflowing with laughter and geniuses, and I
was never bored.*

Your letters fed my sorrow. You wrote long, flowery missives, the envelopes full of little things—feathers, autumn leaves, and then, at the end of the first year, which is perhaps when you understood I had no plans to return, you began sending me paintings. I hung them one after the other on the walls of my office, and it felt rather as if you'd been standing there with me all that time, as if you'd sent your artifacts as envoys to keep an eye on me. Sometimes one of my colleagues would let his gaze wander while I was looking for something, and I could see him blink, lean closer to a canvas, and eventually say, "Forgive me for being nosy, but . . . is this a Frank Appledore?"

And when I said yes, simply because it was true, I could count to ten until I saw his eyes grow wider still when he realized that *everything* in that office was by Frank Appledore. *Except me*, I dared add on occasion as a joke, until I understood that no one ever laughed, because by then no one was listening to me anymore. No matter who happened to be in my office at the time—professor, printer, journalist, friend, writer—he or she would take several minutes to return to reality, first turning their head in silence, almost religiously, motionless in the middle of my office. They would crane their neck towards the smaller paintings, or dare to go right up to them, sometimes even taking hold of them. I learned to be as patient as a museum attendant. All these Appledores, gathered here so unexpectedly. I imagine it was a bit of a shock to suddenly realize this. And then, they were such astonishing canvases, immediately recognizable as authentic, but they nevertheless seemed to belong to a separate branch of your production, like some newly-discovered animal species, existing as a whole in my office in Back Bay. I even had to have an alarm system installed, after I foolishly let the editor-in-chief of a magazine persuade me to pose for my portrait there—excellent publicity, but a genuine risk. The portrait was used again later in books about your work, because of the little collection's fascinating effect. Someone wrote somewhere that it was an oeuvre in and of itself—an original Appledore creation, one of a kind, assembled through multiple postal dispatches, miles from the artist's location—which meant he had not been able to determine the disposition of the paintings, but had nevertheless conceived of the work as a whole. Thus I, Helen, was an instrument among others, in this matter—a sure medium, someone sufficiently close to you to have instinctively understood that I must not separate the various pieces you sent me; someone, too, whom you apparently trusted so completely that you had never needed to come and see your work *in situ*, as if you had been sure all along that it would meet your expectations. The Frank Appledore who tormented curators as a rule, who would take a tape measure from his pocket to measure the space between canvases at the slightest provocation, who would sleep on a camp bed among his paintings during the run-up to an exhibition out of superstition: this same Frank Appledore never felt the need to come and see what he had constructed in my office, on the other side of the Atlantic Ocean.

Y et that was not what really upset me—neither your demonstration of skill, nor your intruding on tip-toe into my territory—no. It was your absence. Your blatant absence, Frank, all those years I lived in Boston. You never, ever, came to see me. You went everywhere else. Venice. Tokyo. San Francisco. Moscow. You traveled so much that you were even frequently away when I went back to Europe for a spell. Your schedule seemed to be absolutely out of control, and as a result we rarely saw each other, for almost five years, in fact. Letters, packages, telephone calls, a few late-night dinners in improbable places and which always seemed to go by in a flash, and that was all. When I think back, it was as if you were avoiding me, either because you didn't want me to see the conditions you were living in at the time—your flat, your friends, kept well away from me for the first time in our lives, or because you were afraid of me, in some way, and were keeping me at a distance, as if I were some dangerous thing, radioactive with marriage: a wife. You did not seem to have room for that sort of outmoded thing in your life, even when it was your oldest friend simply wearing a little rose-gold ring on her left hand. Clearly, there was something going on, even though you never acknowledged it: Günther's wife could no longer be yours, and was anything but. *You look like your mother, or mine,* you wrote, systematically, if I made the mistake of sending you a few photographs. That was not true, of course—how greatly I did *not* resemble my mother was something I had found out at my cost, and I certainly did not resemble Kate either—and I often wondered if all you meant was that I had reached the age our mothers had been when we began to look at them, to *see* them, really see them, for the first time, lucidly. Is that what had driven my best friend to avoid me, unfairly, when I was in my forties: the resurgence of the memory of our parents? You would, however, come to accept it later on—better still, you yourself would end up looking just like Horatio. It was extraordinary, in the space of merely a year, which today I cannot possibly put a precise date on—but in the beginning, with your exacerbated selfishness, you were apparently perfectly happy to shut me out. *You look like our mothers, you look like our mothers, you look like our mothers.* Scribbled countless times on your letters, enhanced with smiling little faces to soften the insult. Yet you got it wrong. I might be the age of our mothers, there was no getting around it—but I was also, indisputably, *not* a mother.

I suppose it was planned, but I have tried so hard to forget it that now I have trouble remembering. I wanted—I wanted a child with my husband. I didn't even think about it as something I desired, but rather as something that was simply my due, a stage I could not help but attain. Of course, I knew I was nearing forty, and that I had not got pregnant even once in a quarter century of active sex life—but I still thought, naively, that it was a dream within my reach, the banal fulfillment of my condition as a mammal. I began dreaming of a child. I thought about it all the time. It was the first thing I thought about upon waking, the last thing before going to bed. I embroidered baby clothes. I made lists of names that I read out loud when I was alone. Three times I carried a child, but not a single one survived beyond the fourth month of pregnancy. Sometimes, back then, I would happen to hear pregnant women complaining of their loss of freedom, having to forswear alcohol or cancel their holidays, and I would feel like killing someone. But over time I came to accept the fact that I would end up the only one of my kind, the last of my line, the orphaned youngest sibling, the survivor of my parents and my idiotic brothers. Günther accepted our failure to have children with his usual discernment. When we received the final medical verdict, he took me out to dinner at our favorite restaurant, he told me he didn't need a child with me in order to love me, and afterwards, for weeks, he sent flowers to my office, all sorts of flowers, until I told him that he could stop. He was someone I could say things like that to, who understood. He stopped talking about children, and I even suspected him, at times, of refraining from making a fuss over a child in my presence, to protect me from the illusory image of my dream. What I mean is that infertility did not come between us—in any case, did not drive us any further apart than we already were, for other reasons. We could have gone on living like that forever, I suppose—getting along well, respecting each other's freedom, sharing the apartment, pursuing our glorious careers. Two adults who had reached the age of wisdom, with fascinating careers and a comfortable income at their disposal, in a splendid part of the world. Yet there were times I had urges to escape, and it was then that I began running. In December that year John Lennon was murdered outside his home, the Dakota Building in New York, and everywhere around me his voice began to resonate. *I was dreaming of the past, and my heart was beating fast, I began to lose control, I began to lose control.*

I t was during my fifth year in Boston that a strange rumor
reached my ears, to the effect that on numerous occasions
you had been seen holding a child by the hand. Urgently
crossing the Atlantic Ocean, so it seemed, all the way from
Amsterdam to me, the details of these sightings constantly con-
tradicted one another: some said it was a little girl, others a little boy, roughly two years old, or perhaps four—but they all
tallied on one point: there was something new in the kingdom
of Appledore.

E ventually someone took photographs of you and the child on the sly, and someone else sent them to me, and as I examined them through the gold-rimmed magnifying glass you had given me as a joke on my twenty-third birthday, I was better able to understand people's reactions. The child—a boy, according to my own estimations, which would turn out to be correct—was a miniature you; he had your green eyes and brown hair, and your demeanor, and several pictures showed you together at parties or gallery openings, and you were, how to put it, extremely well-matched, it was truly disturbing, the child was dressed like a child, with striped T-shirts or sweat-shirts, he couldn't have been more than three or four years old, yet he seemed extraordinarily calm and mysterious. In my favorite pictures in the series that was sent to me back then, you are at a desk signing something, while the little boy is lying on the floor and drawing with markers on a sheet of white paper. People who had known us long before called me to ask for more information, but I hadn't a clue. I too was in a state of shock, and I didn't dare formulate what seemed to me the most likely hypothesis, but also the most disgraceful—that through some means I knew nothing about, you had procured this new accessory, this captivating *doppelgänger*, and it was nothing more than another strategy for you to control your image. It was so effective, so masterful, that it made me forget that only one thing on earth can produce such an emotion: the truth. After many tormented, questioning nights, trying to get to the bottom of the enigma, I eventually rang you from across the Atlantic. It was not easy to get hold of you, the phone would ring and ring as if in a void, but after several dozen fruitless attempts I finally got you, and wasting no time saying my name—you always recognized my voice on the telephone, within a split-second—I asked you:

"Frank, who is that child?"

"He's mine, obviously," was all you said.

In the two hours we spent on the phone that day, you told me a bit more. The little boy's name was Ludwig, and he was born of a brief affair you'd had three years earlier with a young German dancer by the name of Freja, and at the time you knew nothing about it. She'd already left on tour with her ballet company when she realized she was pregnant, and apparently she decided not to tell you. All that time, she had been bringing your son up by herself, taking him everywhere with her, all over Europe, wherever her commitments led her. It was only recently that you received an unexpected letter from Freja's mother informing you all at once of both your fatherhood and Freja's death in a "domestic accident"—a heroin overdose, in fact. In a state of shock, you expressed your desire to take the child in, and you went to Saarbrücken to meet him, and adored him the moment you saw him. You went through the necessary formalities to make him legally yours, took him home with you, and that was where matters stood at present. You insisted that your reunion—or *union, rather*, you said, with a nervous little laugh—had gone smoothly, and that the two of you had a lot of fun together.

"I honestly think I haven't felt this good in ages. He speaks an odd mixture of German and English, he picked up bits of both languages when Freja was on tour, I suppose, so it's almost like an imaginary language, his accent is impossible, it's wonderful. He wasn't part of the plan, at all, but now I want to take care of him."

You went on, and on, and from miles away I listened, spell-bound, curled up on the black velvet sofa Günther had given me for our third wedding anniversary. Before I hung up you invited me to come for a visit to meet little Ludwig, and that was how I ended up on a flight to Amsterdam, off to see the two of you without further delay.

Y ou came to meet me at the airport, and it was my first
    and enduring image of Ludwig: a little boy with green
    eyes and tousled brown hair, who watched me walking
towards him, and once I was standing there before him he said,
in a tiny little voice:

"Are you my mother?"

I know what you told me, Frank. That when you went to get him, two months earlier, at his maternal grandmother's in Saarbrücken, there was only one book in his suitcase, a classic by P.D. Eastman, in which a baby bird goes off looking for its mother, and questions in succession a kitten, a hen, a dog, a cow, a boat, and an airplane. *Are you my mother?*—it wasn't a real question, just the title of the book. I know that. I also read it to your child, dozens of times. I often wondered how it had ended up in his hands, or why it hadn't been taken from him after Freja died, since the text was such a painful reminder of his own experience. *Where am I? asks the little bird. I want to go home! I want my mother!* Reading these words out loud to a three-year-old half-orphan. Reading them several nights in a row. And reading them without crying. But I digress. What I am trying to say, Frank, is that I remember what you told me—it was the title of a children's book—a book Ludwig was very fond of. He wasn't asking me a question. He was simply reciting his book. But in spite of everything, you see, I cannot get the scene out of my mind. One day, in the huge arrivals hall at Schiphol, a little boy who was your spitting image came up to me and said:

"Are you my mother?"

On the last page, the little bird finds its mother, and most oddly, his mother asks him, *Do you know who I am? Yes,* says the little bird, bravely. *I know who you are. You're not a kitten, you're not a hen, you're not a dog, you're not a cow, you're not a boat, and you're not an airplane. You're a bird and you're my mother.*

We took a taxi together from the airport to what was the eleventh flat you'd rented on your own since my departure, and where Ludwig had already been living with you for two months. He had his own room, a spacious, luminous room you had decorated with collages all over the walls, and it was incredibly beautiful—but it wasn't enough. The little boy's room was like an enclave, *a Vatican*, I thought, stunned, in the middle of the permanent battlefield of your everyday life. You had hired a cleaning man, a student who viewed himself as your disciple, and you probably could have asked this young man to do anything for you, although clearly not the laundry. You didn't hire a babysitter, because you were proud of being able to look after your son on your own, but in reality, you were unable to set aside the time required. More often than not you were in your studio painting, as always, listening to music while Ludwig drifted around you, completely disoriented. And there were too many people coming and going—the guests at endless boozy dinners, friends bursting in without knocking, journalists there to interview you, and in the midst of all that, this poor little boy, out of place, completely distraught, with his ragged fluffy lion and his colored pencils nibbled down to the lead. Until then I hadn't a clue of what your life had been like since my departure. You had sent me your change of address whenever you moved, in your letters you had described what you were up to, but all that time I only had *your* version of reality, and I had underestimated how much our paths had diverged over these few years. One way or another, the fact of sharing my life with Günther had given it a certain armor. I had always been more serious than you, and my time with him had made me even more subdued. All the years I had spent not looking after you, nearly a decade, I'd put to good use, becoming even more efficient, even more precise. Sitting in your kitchen on the day I arrived I initially felt woefully out of place, but bit by bit my protective reflexes came rushing back.

"This is no good," I said to you, after two glasses of wine. "You can't be thinking of raising your son the way our parents raised us, dragging him around wherever your life's troubles happen to lead you? He didn't ask to be here. You owe him something better than this."

When I mentioned our parents, you frowned, and I knew I'd hit home.

"Fine," you said. "But what do you suggest? This is the first time I've had a child, after all. I don't really know how to go about it."

"For a start, you'll have to move. It's much too chaotic here. Do you have any idea where you could go to live?"

That was when, for the first time, you told me about the house in Normandy.

Y ou had bought the house on a whim, six years earlier, alone at the wheel one day on your way back from Paimpol. In a foul mood after yet another argument with your mother, you had unintentionally strayed off the main road to find yourself in the Norman countryside. Jaw clenched as you drove down the little back roads of Le Perche, you saw the "For Sale" sign from far away, across the hills, and you went to have a look—solely, you said, to clear your mind after your visit with Kate, to calm your hostile thoughts. The house was in good condition, surrounded by an estate vast enough for one to ignore the neighbors, yet only a dozen kilometers or so from a small town—or so you were told by the owners, a couple, as they led you through the rooms. On the ground floor were the kitchen, a living room with a fireplace, and a dining room with multiple windows looking out on a grassy slope below. On the second floor, there were two bathrooms and six sunny bedrooms, not to mention the attic on the third floor, which had been renovated. Most importantly, there were two more independent outbuildings in addition to the main building: a small shed where we would eventually keep the firewood, and a huge wooden barn, where you would set up your studio. It was the barn that had swayed you, you told me—the barn and the very reasonable asking price for the entire property. After the tour, you made an offer, between two cups of milky tea with the owners; you rang your solicitor when you got home, and the matter was settled very quickly, all you had to do was sign the papers you received in the post. At first you thought you would be going to your new domain on a regular basis. You had acquired it with an image of yourself driving on your own to your secret haven, shutting yourself away one week a month to work in the peace and quiet of your barn, then heading back to the city, whistling at the wheel, the car filled with wonderful pictures—but it didn't happen. You never went there. You were caught up in the high life of parties, exhibitions, and trips abroad. At first light, you often promised your fellow revelers memorable weekends by the fire drinking aged French liqueurs, and to your women, all your women without distinction, you held out the alluring prospect of torrid romantic interludes amid apple tarts, flowered rooms, and torrential downpours—but in the end, you did not take anyone to Normandy. You had, in fact, almost forgotten about your house, and it was only when I pointed out that you needed to get away from the city for the welfare of your son that you remembered your property lost in the middle of the Norman forests, and after a quick trip there together to check it out, I persuaded you to move there with the little boy.

I don't know exactly when, in the midst of all this, we decided that I should come along. Perhaps we never really did decide, in the end—and it was this lack of clarity that eventually turned against us. At the beginning of 1981, I stayed in Amsterdam for two months and helped you pack up and say your goodbyes, I lent a hand with all the various details of the move; we bought furniture, sheets, and dishes, and in the end, without further ado, I boarded a flight to inform Günther that I was leaving him and was going to live with you and your son in the Norman countryside.

Our marriage had been on the skids for several years, and the fact we'd been apart all that time while I was in Europe convinced me that the two of us no longer had a future together. Naturally, it was more complicated than that, more mysterious—to be living with you again in your messy flat, even for only a few weeks, had been incredibly sweet, as if at last I could breathe again. I had felt at home, perfectly myself, for the first time in years. I thought I bore some responsibility in the matter—that if I hadn't gone off and left you to your fate by getting married, things would have turned out differently, and the least I could do now was stay by your side and help raise your son. Who else, other than me, I thought, could have, should have been there? On some level, surely, I was kidding myself, exaggerating my own importance, making myself feel needed. I imagined that without my protective presence you would *never* manage, that Ludwig would grow up surrounded by a multitude of dangerously incompetent stepmothers, and I alone would be capable of erecting a life-saving barrier against them. And yet it was true, in a way— just how far I was prepared to go remained to be seen, but surely, I was wrong to think the situation was set in stone. At the time, however, my options did seem perfectly clear: leave my husband to be with you, go and live with you in a part of France I knew nothing about, assume responsibility for a child who was not my own, and throw myself headlong into a new life which would be very similar to the old one. I would undoubtedly have reacted in a completely different way had I been satisfied with my own life—but that simply wasn't the case. After our quick trip to Normandy to see the house, I had made my decision. Like most people, what I knew of France was principally Paris, but I fell in love with Normandy at first sight. There it was, the house of my dreams, the one I had missed so much from my glass penthouse in Boston: a cen-turies-old house, with bramble bushes and a well, with shadows and hidden recesses. A rose bush climbing the facade, and countryside as far as the eye could see. I would get my way. But you were delighted, too—relieved and happy. Once again, I'd appeared as if by magic and was coming to your rescue, the way I had twenty-five years earlier, to help you run away to Amsterdam, and this time I'd come, right on time, to help you with the burden of your new responsibility. In the few weeks we spent getting ready to move, you were constantly *brandishing* me, literally, before all your friends, and proclaiming:

"Helen is back, she'll take care of everything!"

Your childish selfishness, which always drove you to blithely disregard anything that did not concern you directly, made you miss something that was, nevertheless absolutely fundamental: the very reasons for my return. All you saw were your own interests, you were content with the knowledge that I had come back to "take care of everything," but apparently you never wondered what could have caused me to leave so abruptly the man who had been my husband for five reason-ably sweet years, not to mention the country where I had been working all that time, and my American life—in short, to become your Mary Poppins. It was something *you* could have done—you bought houses in Normandy on a whim—so it must have seemed normal to you. You didn't pick up on the fact that my decision was not at all my usual style, and in my case, could mean only one thing: that I had an excellent reason for what I was doing.

I had never stopped missing you, and so the prospect of living near you again was a factor, naturally. Moreover, my marriage was in a nose-dive. At forty-two, I was too young to be unhappy, was how I saw it. I had put all my heart into the marriage, but it hadn't worked. And then, well, as you know, I'm conservative: any charm Boston had laboriously managed to acquire for me, in the end, melted away when set against my older attachment to the unforgettable texture of the long years we had spent together. Nostalgia has always been a sort of religion to me. But there was something *new*, as well. Inexplicably, fate had just given you what I wanted more than anything: a child. You found the very concept of motherhood so dreadful that you were none the wiser, and I never heard you use a single word from the lexicon of motherhood. Behind all mothers lay your abhorrence of your own. Freja's death was surely the only circumstance that could have induced you to have a child. And even when I came to live with you, even when the image of a family was cast before us on the asphalt of Le Perche by our three shadows, you never realized that I was there for your child. Like those fairies in tales who come to exchange their horrid offspring for the man-cub they will wrench from his cradle in the night, I had come to exchange my barrenness and my failed marriage for a warm spot in your luminous life.

W hen I told him I was leaving him, Günther did not protest. I had come to the apartment without warning. I had gone straight to our room and begun packing. When I think back, I am ashamed of my eagerness. He was my husband, after all—a charming man I had married of my own free will, and I could have been more gracious on leaving him. When he returned from work he came into the bedroom and saw me there, tossing all my belongings into suitcases, willy-nilly, and he gave a weak smile and said,

"Where are you going like this, Helen?"

"Normandy," I said.

"With Frank, then?"

"Yes."

Never raising his voice, Günther uttered a few striking words of regret, and for a brief instant I was reminded of how desirable his calm manner had seemed to me compared to your outbursts, once I had decided to marry him, only a few years earlier. But I instantly banished the thought. I'd made my decision. I was going to go back and live with you, and take control of my life. In silence, I gathered my things, folded my clothes, piled my books into boxes, and left the house.

One week after I arrived in Amsterdam, while we were still sorting a few practical details before leaving for Normandy for good, I received a letter from Günther.

Helen,

People often forget what elevators are, how they made skyscrapers possible. There's a long history to elevators. But since you didn't ask me my opinion before you took off, I will take the liberty of telling you the following story. You're not obliged to read it, of course. You will do as you please, as always.

Archimedes invented the winch. Later, in the year 80 B.C., the Romans were already using hoists to take gladiators and wild beasts up to the level of the arena, and then, of course, in the middle of the nineteenth century, there was Thompson's hydraulic lift. But it was not until 1852 that Elisha Graves Otis designed the first safety elevator, in Yonkers, in southern New York State. The first model was inaugurated five years later in a shop that sold porcelain and French glassware. In the years that followed, Otis perfected his device, and it was this new technology that allowed for the development of ever higher floors, and thus the considerable increase in the height of construction, which thus far had been limited to brick buildings that were not authorized to surpass twelve stories. But in 1885, with the birth of metal framework, there were no longer any barriers to the ambition of architects, and the elevator allowed them to reach for the highest summits. You are probably wondering what I'm getting at with all this. In a similar fashion, you are the one who made Frank possible. And as with the role of elevators in the history of skyscrapers—I'm afraid no one ever talks about it.

Farewell, my love.

NORMANDY

A re we going to live here, now?" Ludwig asked gravely, the night we moved, as he sat on his new little bed in his new bedroom.

"Yes."

"Why?"

"Because we think it's a good idea."

"Who's we?"

"Your daddy and I."

"Are all three of us going to live together now?"

"Yes."

He remained silent for a few moments, as if he were weighing the pertinence of this information, and then he said, "Why is it a good idea to be here?"

Ludwig was probably both anxious and curious about this new situation, but that evening I was pure elation. I had spent the day opening boxes with a cutter and putting things away in the furniture that had been delivered a few weeks earlier. I loved it all—the smell of old stones and new wood, the rooms I was mentally making my own by walking to and fro with armfuls of belongings. The house seemed even more beautiful than the first time I had visited. And now I was sitting on the edge of the child's bed I had carefully chosen from a catalogue for Ludwig—a storage bed with deep drawers where I imagined he would very soon put his most precious treasures. I leaned over him and stroked his hair, I felt incredibly good, I could do anything. But he was too young for me to tell him our story—

yours and mine—still too young to understand the miracle of our being together again, in this extraordinary place. When he had questioned me, I had hunted for an appropriate answer, one that would reassure him, and because I had let my gaze wander dreamily over to the window, I saw the edge of the forest of Le Perche at the end of our drive, with its verdant springtime trees, its disarming presence, and the words practically slipped out.

"Because there are trees."

That's exactly what I said.

On the first night after we moved in, I heard you give a light tap at my door.

"Helen? It's me. Can you open?"

I jumped out of bed and went to open the door. You were wearing only your pajama bottoms and your chest was bare. You were smiling, the enamel of your teeth gleaming in the darkness. I stepped back to let you in, and you put your arms around me. It all came back, all at once. My wounded, sixteen-year-old self, your room in the embassy. Amsterdam. The smell of soy. The trip to Italy, when we were twenty-eight. And then your skin, the smell of your hair when you picked me up to carry me to the bed. It was you. It was you, Frank Appledore, my best friend, my heart. The two of us hadn't made love for over ten years, and it was as if time had stopped. When I came, my orgasm reverberated like a huge bronze bell.

In the days that followed, I could not keep myself from observing you. You had the same smell, but not the same voice. You drank more, but you'd stopped smoking—only now and again, where no one could see you, or so you thought, you relapsed, and I could make out the glow of a cigarette in the darkness of the garden, yet I could not determine what prompted these lapses. But it was psychologically that you had changed, more than anything. When I boarded my plane for America five years earlier, I was leaving behind a turbulent man in his thirties, in his artistic prime, and now I had returned to a wily man in his forties, with copper skin, muted gestures, and bare feet. At the time, I didn't go back to living with you on the assumption that at last we would fall deeply in love—no. But I do suppose I saw our lovemaking that first night as a good sign—more than that. I was like a beggar for love, I simply, desperately wanted someone to touch me. I did, however, take a dim view of the way you flirted with the babysitter we sometimes hired for the end of the day, so we would each have time to work in our respective studies—a local girl, scarcely out of adolescence, the round-faced baker's daughter from the next village. Her name was Elsa, but Ludwig called her Zaza, so we called her Zaza, too. I don't know why I've brought this up. More than once I saw you talking to her out on the sunny terrace, then you would lead her by the hand into your studio to show her your canvases, the pictures you had painted, some of them before she was even born, and I felt sorry for you, because she hadn't a clue who you were, and from the window opposite my desk I could read your lips as you tried to explain to her, *I'm Frank Appledore, I'm an artist, I've done this, and this, and this, too*—and she didn't understand a thing, she smiled at you calmly, as if to comfort you. She didn't need to know who you were, however, to agree to listen to you. Your leonine beauty, at forty-three, with your charm intact, your energy, your very strangeness; and it could be, too, that you had made a strong impression on this girl—who had probably never left her native region—because of the sizeable estate you owned here: all your attributes put together were enough to move her to please you, however little she understood. You had put on a bit of weight, in those days, particularly because moving to the country had brought a halt to your consumption of drugs, something I was not fully aware of at the time, and you were beginning to bear an unsettling resemblance to your father. You were still the same Frank, in spite of everything, still a child or a king who left crumbs on the floor and didn't close drawers, who didn't reply when he was called to dinner, who only half listened and always went back to dwelling on his own obsessions, who scattered paperwork all over the house in the altogether realistic hope that when I picked them up I would also fill them out, update them, and send them on to whom it might concern; you were still the same stubborn individual who refused to see a doctor when you coughed, refused to change your trousers even when they were so stiff with paint they cracked when you bent your knees, refused to wash your hair, to plan ahead, to take those around you into consideration. But I had been nestling in that hollow in your temperament since the age of twelve. There was nothing more familiar to me. When I whirled around the house picking up the things—shoes, paintbrushes, tax forms—you'd scattered in your wake like some feral creature, things I would put neatly back where they belonged, I felt a surge of intense well-being. It had always been up to me to know where things were. I was the one, no one else, who decided where they belonged. I told Zaza that we were no longer in need of her services.

In the years we spent in Normandy, something else happened that was very important. You began painting the forest. Oak, beech, chestnut, sycamore maple, wild cherry, linden, aspen, hornbeam, rowan, birch, willow, elderberry, hazel, crab apple and wild pear, as well as the ground you scrutinized when you went mushroom-picking. Initially you made pencil drawings: squares of humus, dead leaves and twigs, insects, feathers lost by careless birds. Then you painted landscapes. When I drove our estate car down the little roads, I could see you in the distance, beyond the hills, standing here or there in a meadow with your easel, initially next to the cows, looking at the forest *from the outside*; then, as the weeks went by, you moved closer to its depths, beginning at the foot of the first trees, then advancing into the undergrowth, the clearings, to the very heart of the great national forest. Not for a very long time had anyone placed nature at the heart of their art in this way. There had been Courbet, the blessed son of the Franche-Comté, with his incredible *Oak at Flagey* and any number of stunning landscapes—Courbet, the first master, and then, much later, there were Van Gogh's cypress trees, too, and Klimt's birches, Monet's poplars, Mondrian's apple trees, and now you, Frank Appledore, heading out every morning with your box of paints and your silence, wrapped up in your military surplus jacket, a sandwich turning to crumbs deep in your pocket; with your lust for life. In the evening when you returned, you had twigs in your hair, you smelled sweetly of smoke, and in a way the simple fact of seeing you in your wellies was reassuring—they were the symbol of a new life, these boots that would have been pointless in the hectic life you had left behind in Amsterdam, although I had offered you Amsterdam on a silver platter twenty-five years earlier, not knowing what would come of it. Those boots said, *I'm at work, and nothing is more important to me now,* they said that you'd had your fill of young models and wild parties and cocktails before noon. The time had come for thick brown bread marked with a cross before it was sliced, for pinches of salt tossed over one's shoulder to ward off misfortune, for logs added to the fire without a word, for fruit baked in red wine in the oven. It was a time for fingernails gritty with earth, for deep sleep, dried roses, long books, beds with creaking springs. You had changed a great deal over the years, but with each passing day in the house in Normandy I saw you begin to resemble yourself again, to grow closer again to the adolescent boy I had known so long ago, with his silence and his passion, his uncon-cern, his stubbornness, his obscene good health. It was as if I'd been tugging you upwards with a rope, grimly, steadily, fathom upon fathom, to save you from drowning. I was proud of what I was accomplishing: your return to the land of Calm. My own return to that land, too. I didn't say as much, perhaps simply because, apart from you and little Ludwig, for a long time I had no one to talk to in our place of exile—but I felt a resplen-dent peacefulness. My mind was as clear as a mountain lake. I confronted each new day—no, better than that, I created each new day, instead of enduring them as I seemed to have done for so long. The contrast with my state in Boston was so great that I could easily believe I'd been cured of some insidious dis-ease. I felt as if I were getting younger, lighter. I would press my palm on the tin pastry cutter to make little bunnies in the dough, and then Ludwig and I would decorate them with tiny brushes and food coloring; I planted flowers in the garden, squeezing my thumb into the soft crumbly chocolate brown soil, and when I went with my apron under my mac to call you to lunch, knocking at the door of the studio-barn where you were working, I was in incredibly good spirits, as if at last I had managed to catch up with my own life, as if there were not miles and years separating this ancient great oak door and the vaguely Japanese panel that slid open onto your first studio in Amsterdam. In the barn your palette continually evolved, gold and garnet had replaced the blues and greens of your early years, autumn was coming, Ludwig was four years old, making his own herbaria, and we were very happy.

"I think this is why I didn't come and settle here any earlier," you said. "I wasn't ready for this major work. I knew it was waiting for me here."

In 1982, the year Gabriel García Márquez was awarded the Nobel Prize for literature, we celebrated our first full year in the country. On the anniversary of our moving in I spent the day simmering a *coda alla vaccinara*, one of your favorite Roman dishes, made with oxtail, pancetta, celery, and raisins. I sent Ludwig to bed early with his collection of Beatrix Potter books, I spread a magnificent linen tablecloth on the dining table, put on an evening gown with a heart-shaped neckline, opened a bottle of wine, and we had dinner just the two of us.

"It's been a good year, hasn't it?" I said timidly, shortly before dessert, in the glow of two silver candlesticks.

"Excellent," you said, pushing your chair back to stretch your legs. "You did the right thing, making us come here. I've never done such good work."

"And Ludwig is doing well, don't you think?"

"Yes. He has been literally glowing since we came here. It's such a relief to see him like this. I can never thank you enough for all you've done for us, you know."

My face was flushed with a golden warmth from the candles, so I don't think you saw me blush.

"Do you know why he was called Ludwig, actually?" I asked.

"His mother loved Beethoven."

"How could you possibly know that?" I said, blithely surprised. "You were only with her for one night."

"Not exactly."

"But you said—"

"I know what I said. At the time, it seemed simpler. But that wasn't the whole truth."

You looked at me.

"If I tell you, Helen, do you promise to keep my secret?"

"I'm your best friend, aren't I?"

And so, across the cluttered table, you gave me the true version of the story you'd told me the first time around. The major difference was that Freja was not at all a one-night-stand who had hidden her pregnancy from you. You had been seeing her for months, you had lived with her in Amsterdam, and you had left her when she told you she was pregnant. The first time you explained this, I wasn't sure I had quite grasped what you were saying, and I remember asking, incredulously:

"Did you leave her because she was taking drugs? Was that it?"

"No."

You laughed, and then you continued:

"Honestly, Helen. It was the seventies. I don't know what it was like in Boston, but here in Europe, if you left someone because they were doing drugs, you wouldn't know a soul. No, I left her because I didn't want a child with her. I told her as much. I was dead clear about it. She tried to trap me, but I was having none of it."

"But then when Ludwig was born, did you know about it?"

"Yes."

"And you didn't want to go and see him? You didn't talk with her about him?"

"No, no. I'd made my point."

I'd been drinking wine, and cognac, but my drunkenness could not quite soften the blow of what you were telling me. There I'd been in Boston, desperately trying to get pregnant, while you'd fathered a child by accident and then gone and abandoned him. You had known of Ludwig's existence right from the start, but you'd preferred to disregard the information. This marvelous child, whom I loved passionately: you had rejected him without a qualm.

A nd in the end, the fact that you shared your secret with me, despite its poisonous nature, seemed to strengthen my sense that I'd made the right decision, that I was vital to you, and to Ludwig. I suppose some part of me had known intrinsically, from the start, that I had no business there, that it was not my place, that I had come for the wrong reasons—and so to discover that you, too, had something to hide: this reassured me, and I liked it. Suddenly it all became so perfectly clear: the stone house, the green countryside, the little boy, the barn full of artwork, you with your catastrophic lie, this terrible thing you had done to a very young woman and to your infant child, these terrible things you were still capable of saying about it even to this day; and me, the confusion in my mind, and all my bad feelings. We were even. Sometimes, briefly, I had the sensation that we'd become the doubles of our fathers—living together for all the wrong reasons. If our twenties were a time of self-delusion, our fifties, which we were fast approaching, threatened to be the era of harsh clarity. When you told me the truth about Freja and Ludwig, you didn't try to make me believe that things were not as serious as they seemed. You no longer needed to justify yourself, after all. You were Frank Appledore. For years now you'd no longer had to do any-thing you disliked—for years you hadn't been forced to do anything. Whether it was rejecting Freja, or sending something back at a restaurant, or lying over the phone to get out of an appointment which, at the last minute, you no longer wanted to keep—was there any difference? You had clearly told her *no*, unambiguously explained that if she kept the child, she would be on her own. You had even offered to pay for an abortion. You would have sent her money if it had been a question of money, of course, you would have paid child support, but she disappeared without leaving an address, and you didn't want to seem inconsistent by starting to look for her. Nor was it your fault if she subsequently died, leaving behind this wonderful little boy. Over and over you said, as if to give a rhythm to your story, *I didn't want to have* a family *with Freja*, while I—this I now know—I heard this affirmation as meaning, with Freja, no, but with me, Helen, yes.

Ten years later we were still there, and I was in my fifties. I was in fine form. I would do gymnastics as soon as I got out of bed, I'd rigged a trapeze from a beam in the bedroom for stretching, and I ran for an hour every day, through the forest surrounding the property. I went running come rain or shine, and I ran fast. The ability to run for a long time is one of the rare human gifts that does not diminish with age, an unexpected legacy of the first humans, who had to run for miles to tire their prey in order to catch them, because we are the only species of mammal that are able to adjust our body temperature through sweat—hunter-gatherers were no match for the antelopes and wart hogs they coveted, but apparently as a tribe they could track them for hours—men, women, children, and the elderly all running to converge at the kill, and share their feast wherever the hunt had led them. Hundreds of centuries after those pre-historical times, on carefully surfaced roads through the French forest, I was running in my fifties without losing my breath, I could feel all my muscles working, the soles of my feet, the suppleness of my toes, my flat belly, my taut thighs, amid the rustling of leaves and the agitation of birds, the cracking of branches and the hard fruits thudding to the ground as they fell from the treetops. The beauty of the forest is never as visible as when one stands on its edge, when one's gaze believes it is taking in all the depth of the forest, observing the rays of powdery light as they slice through the branches, and there was something primitive about this forest, with its huge Douglas pines, and the centuries-old oaks where I expected at any moment to see warriors dressed in heavy furs, their weapons brandished. I'd forgotten Boston ever existed. Putting my two little feet on the soil of Europe seemed to have been enough to rouse me from my long sleep. I was full of energy, I carried wood to the shed, I cleared cartloads of brambles, I picked fruit, I felt powerful and fulfilled—no doubt because I was. But there was something else: the fact of living with you again, of having picked up the thread of our long life together, that made me forget about my age. In a way, by being together, we were still the children we had been. As if our friendship—how strange that word sounds!—had trans-fixed us, immobilized us in a moment of calm.

B eing with you took me back to a period of childhood that, without my being able to do anything about it, probably left me incapable of being a parent worthy of the name. We had a child, and we had no idea what was best for him. No one had ever taught us anything about children, after all. All throughout our own childhood we'd been carted here and there, never receiving any tenderness, and in our dissolute lives that followed we hadn't spent any time with children, so I have sometimes wondered if that was why we failed so miserably in that domain. Ludwig had no one but us, and we were incapable of honoring that fact, for reasons that are ours alone. I swear I did my best—but deep down I think my best was worthless, my best would, in any case, never have been enough, because I had nothing to show anyone save my own astonishment, my own stupor when it came to the world, a world I'd spent my life fleeing from, in books. I could set aside time, I could make myself available, which I did, but what could I teach a newcomer? I fed him, bought him books, helped him with his homework, gave him hugs, and I loved him, with all my heart, but how could I show him the path to follow, make life easier for him, when I had always, or nearly always, lived alone with one and the same person, the only person I'd ever succeeded in understanding in half a century on the planet? And that person whom I thought I understood so well: that person understood him, Ludwig, so poorly, could make nothing of his questions, his doubts; how could the two of us have given him a home fit to live in? Remember? The morning he turned seven, when I was leaning over his bed and asking what would make him happy for his birthday, Ludwig said he wanted to be with his mother, and when I replied that it wasn't possible, he said, very quietly,

"Yes, Helen, it is possible. If I'm dead. I heard that dead people all go to the same place. If I'm dead I can go there, too."

"I don't think it works quite like that," I said, holding my breath.

A bit later on, when he was up and dressed and sitting in the kitchen with you and a plate of sugared waffles, I went upstairs to shut myself in the laundry cupboard and cry my eyes out. In the years that followed, I thought he'd got over it—his *morbid obsession*, was the way you would put it, all those years, to describe the sadness of your motherless little boy. It's not entirely fair, but there are times I would like to say it was all your fault, it was because of you and your brutal description of things that I was not as mindful as I should have been of the feelings of my adoptive son. While I wept over my helplessness amid the linen, you refused to grant any legitimacy to his sorrow, and between us Ludwig was growing up.

T hose thirteen years went by in a flash. What can I tell you about them that you don't already know? I was happy, nearly every day. I worked, gardened, brought up your little boy, and in the blink of an eye he had become a sweet adolescent. I taught him how to tend the garden and prune the roses. In the meantime, you had embarked on painting your largest works ever. I could smell the solvents from fifteen yards away, and I felt good. That's what they were, for me, those years between 1981 and 1994: gentle rain, jam-making, mushroom omelets, apple tarts, love when the moon was full, the smell of waxed floorboards, your masterpieces in the barn, and my masterpiece of a newly formed family. In the evening, after I got Ludwig to bed, while you were toasting your toes by the fire, I smiled as I listened to the lyrics of a Roy Orbison song that went, *Anything you want, you got it. Anything you need, you got it.* But it was a bit more complicated than that. I was in the thick of the menopause, and I doubt you ever even *thought* about that, Frank. I felt very lonely, at times, when I sprayed myself with hormones to keep my wits about me, when I leafed through medical journals in the middle of the night in search of remedies to my problem, when from one day to the next I was absolutely exhausted and you never even wondered what was wrong, you just asked what was for dinner that evening or had I had time to help Ludwig with his homework, or else you were in a good mood, hopping around me to the strains of some pathetic music, with reserves of energy that were an absolute torment to someone who hadn't had a decent night's sleep in seventy-two hours. You seemed to have withdrawn all consideration towards others for good, you'd stopped even trying, or pretending. All your attention went into your painting—meticulously, you examined the autumn leaves, the moss, the dried fruit, the fences, the animals grazing. You contemplated them, patiently, respectfully, in silence, but you took Ludwig and me utterly for granted, we went without saying, we were incontestable and silent. It always feels a bit petty to criticize an artist for a lack of attention to trivial things, to think, with a shrug of one's mental shoulders, *he only sees what is there before him*, because one knows that, on the contrary, mysteriously, it is the artist who sees, now and forever, the things that escape us, yet which do seem to be the most important—the bones, nerves, and blood of everyday reality, its quintessence, forever beyond our reach as simple mortals—*civilians*, as you used to call them in the old days, when Soto, Ossip and you would refer to people who were not artists. But I was along for the ride—I'd lived with you for years. If I'd known this was my last year with you—1994—I would have been more patient. If I could have seen myself then as I see myself today, if I had known that being able to speak to you would be purely a matter of luck, and that luck alone would bring us together again after an absence of twenty-three years, if I had known that twenty-three years could go by without you, if I had known how long they would be, all these years, if I'd had any inkling of the misfortune that would befall us, Frank, then believe me, I would have done everything differently—everything.

The region eventually adopted us. When I went shopping in the next village, the locals called me Madame Appledore. As embarrassed as I am to confess as much, even today, it is true that I never corrected them, and I never mentioned it to you, either. I thought that since you had almost no contact with the people around there—you relied entirely on me for all our domestic affairs, I don't think you ever bought so much as a light bulb or a croissant or a pair of socks in thirteen years—you would probably never notice, so I could keep this little secret to myself. I suppose I was afraid that if I told you, you would destroy the illusion, you would, once and for all, dispel the charm those two little words had for me. *Madame Appledore*—it was like the final coat of varnish on my grand fabrication. As the villagers themselves had conferred it upon me, it was a consecration, a blessing. Prior to that, I'd had no idea how much I dreamt of being called by your name—is that why I had refused to take Günther's, when I got married? I'll never know, now. But I liked its resonance in French voices, that fine old name meaning *apple tree*, or so your father had explained to me one day, and here it sounded like a particularly judicious mixture of the English and the French: *pomme d'or*, was what I heard when someone called to me from the stalls at the market, *pomme d'or*. And for some unknown reason, I never thought of the futile dispute that had led to the Trojan War, but which had started precisely that way, with a golden apple rolling across the banquet table of the gods, flung there by the goddess of discord. No, Frank, against all expectations, the image that came to me, obsessively, was that of a fairy tale by the Brothers Grimm where the king's youngest daughter plays with a ball of solid gold—the ball falls into a well, and a frog offers the princess a deal: he will return her ball to her if she will allow him, in exchange, to eat from her plate, drink from her goblet, and sleep in her bed. Because she is impatient, the princess agrees and, under pressure from her father, who reminds her that a promise is a promise, she complies, despite her disgust, and in the end the frog is transformed into a handsome young man. During my fairy tale period I wrote about the various versions of this tale, and I suppose something in the tale resonated with me—the notion that the greatest sacrifices lead to the greatest rewards, and so perhaps there was this, too: that if I let you help yourself to what belonged to me, you would eventually kneel beside my bed; but then there was also the image of the golden ball, heavy, lethal, tossed lightly into the air, and threatening—because it would have to fall to the ground again, with all its weight.

And that was exactly what happened, one Monday when, exceptionally, you decided to come to the village with me to do some shopping. I didn't even try to dissuade you—my deceit had been working for years, and like any offender who hasn't been caught red-handed, I'd eventually ended up believing in my own impunity, just as I'd probably ended up believing that the name I'd been given in error was indeed mine. Well, you are no stranger to this sort of thing, I'm not telling you anything new: you too had ended up believing in a number of your own lies, and I was often the one who helped you not to be found out. But the day we went to the village together, you did not know what had been going on behind your back for years. So when the fruit vendor greeted me in her usual manner, you immediately let out a resounding peal of laughter. Nor could you stop laughing, and you said to me, in Italian:

"*Madame Appledore! Dio buono*, Helen, did you hear that?"

Despite the fruit vendor's shocked expression, it never even occurred to you that it might not be the first time—you thought there was some misunderstanding, or a provincial obsession with respectability, the local yokels needing to know what they were supposed to think about us. Better still: because this was one of the rare times you had come to the market, you probably didn't even realize that there had been a market there, in your absence, every Thursday for years. While I may have already been dreading you would find me out one day—

that you would stumble upon my delight in passing myself off as your wife in the valley, and that you would make fun of me—not for one second had I ever imagined what would then ensue. I thought you would be angry. I had not imagined this second option, far worse than the first: you shook with laughter. You really didn't understand. When we got back to the car, our arms full of shopping, you didn't even turn your laughing face towards me when you said:

"*Madame Appledore.* I still can't get over it. They probably take you for my sister, don't you think, Helen? It's like some old Agatha Christie novel: the dark stranger, with his silent spinster sister, moving into a sleepy little village . . . Of course, the sister turns out to be the murderer, in the end."

I did not answer. A few minutes earlier, once you had recovered from your surprise, you had turned to the fruit vendor and said, cheerfully but firmly:

"There is no Madame Appledore."

On a whim, in 1993 we invited Ossip and Soto to celebrate New Year's Eve with us, and fortunately enough they were able to come. One was arriving from New York, the other from Berlin, and suddenly there they were at the end of the drive in a hire car, with two travel bags and the boot filled with paintings and bottles of champagne. I took pictures of the three of you on the terrace, in the faint light of dusk—their clothes are spotted with paint, because you have just hugged one another closely. This wasn't the first time they'd come to visit—both of them had already been here for short stays, but never at the same time, and to see you all together at last had instantly transported me into our happy past. What an extraordinary life we'd had. So much good fortune. The dinner was memorable, rich with laughter; you all told your favorite stories, and Ludwig was hanging on your every word, holding his face in his hands. At the end of the meal he unwound the extension cords to set up his sound system on the terrace, and we danced in our coats, smoking, to the music our son seemed to be shyly offering to us for that special evening. Ludwig didn't dance, he remained seated, concentrating on the order of the songs. While I was dancing to a slow piece with Soto, Soto whispered to me, *I'm so happy for you, Helen. I always thought you were made for each other. It was fate.* The next morning, they left the way they had come. On the first day of 1994, we'd been living in Normandy for thirteen years. We had a vegetable garden, a woodpile, a few beehives. You were continuing your ascension in the art world, feverishly at work in your barn, creating paintings that were destined to make their way all around the world and confirm your reputation. Your tree paintings, Frank, were breathtaking. Everything you have done since has been held to that standard, you know that. I, meanwhile, had become an adoptive daughter of Normandy, speaking French, drinking coffee with Laurence, the neighbor, and working on my books in the silence of the valley. A bit later, in April of that year, the singer of the American rock group whose posters covered the walls in Ludwig's room shot himself dead above the garage at his home in Seattle. As a sort of funeral lament in his honor, Ludwig spent an entire week listening to his albums in his bedroom at night, on repeat, and I could hear the voice of the dead young man resounding dully through the house while I corrected an essay on Henry James.

Come as you are
As you were
As I want you to be
As a friend, as a friend,
As a known enemy.

Death was coming closer, it had found us, but I didn't realize that yet. Several nights a month you would knock at my door, and we made wild love in my cabin bed. It was so extraordinary that I closed my eyes to all the rest. My mistake.

It was at that moment in time that Ludwig's old babysitter, the baker's daughter, suddenly made her reappearance. We hadn't seen her in a number of years. She'd left the region when she was eighteen or so to go and study in Rouen, and as far as I was concerned, she was truly forgotten. Flower buds, apple trees in bloom, late harvest—the seasons had followed one another, and I hadn't given her a moment's thought. But in the summer of 1994 she suddenly came back without warning—twenty-seven or twenty-eight years old now, not so gauche anymore, more resourceful, still just as plump, and very desirable. Her slowness, which had seemed almost pathological to me in the old days, now seemed to have changed into a simmering languor. Her eyes shone with a new awareness of the world, with the experience she'd lacked ten years earlier, and it was as if it had taken all that time for your burning gaze to make its way into her brain and for her to realize, at last, that you used to fancy her. Was that the sole reason she'd come back—who knows? Perhaps, as she walked to work one morning, she was brought to an abrupt halt on the pavement of some *grand boulevard* in Paris when at last her tiny brain laboriously delivered its findings, and she had immediately turned on her heel and headed back to her flat to pack her bags and rush here to tell you yes, now, at last, she had understood. I don't know. But to this day, twenty-three years on, I can see her as clearly as on that morning when she stood in the drizzle in our courtyard, waiting for you to make your way through your studio to come and open the front door to her. Her buttocks in a threadbare pair of Levis, her rubber boots subtly emphasizing the curve of her knees, her bleached blond hair pinned loosely in a chignon, Zaza had come home.

The danger was drawing nearer, but I didn't sense it at once. To me she was still Zaza—a stupid, self-centered kid from whom I purchased precious hours for work, one bright blue fifty-franc note at a time. It was only when I spoke to our neighbor Laurence that I began to see just how much Zaza had changed.

"Elsa is back," said Laurence, opening the door for me when I came for some eggs.

"Yes, I know. But where was she, exactly?" I asked, making friendly conversation while I held out my egg containers for her to fill.

"Paris."

I liked Laurence. I had got to know her during the ten years we'd been neighbors, and every fortnight or so we would invite each other over for coffee and chat about our cuttings. When she said the word "Paris" that day, I noticed she quivered with pleasure in a way I'd never seen.

"Apparently, she was working as an assistant for someone important, and then things took a nasty turn, if you catch my drift, and so she's back here, in the meantime."

"In the meantime until what?"

"Until she finds work, I suppose."

And so, as if I'd finally focused my lenses, I began to have a sharper view of the situation—the young girl from the provinces who'd gone away in triumph to conquer the big city, never looking back, and who'd now been forced into a shamefaced return, which she awkwardly tried to pass off as some tale of sexual harassment in the workplace. Her boredom, her scorn, her rage, the way she clearly hated being forced back to her birthplace. It must have taken colossal reserves of energy for her to carve her niche in Paris, she must have had to get rid of her Norman accent, with its flat syllables, must have had to put the memories of the great forest behind her in order to put up with the huge city—and now here she was back at square one, with all the neighboring villages scrutinizing her with curiosity. Laurence told me she was helping her parents at the bakery on weekends, the way she used to. *Poor Zaza*, I thought, feeling sorry for her—until I saw her that day in the courtyard, waiting patiently for you. That woman was not suffering any hardship. Taking stock of her assets, she'd managed to rebuild something from her anger and shame. She'd been very bored, but as the grown-ups used to tell us when we were little, the devil finds work for idle hands. She had searched, and come up with a plan: mustering all her sex appeal, she prepared to seduce the most fascinating bachelor in the entire valley.

I loved the fresh apples and the red tones of the forest, I loved Ludwig and the house, and the tabby cats from the neighboring farms, and the smell of wood smoke, seemingly trapped forever in the fibers of all my clothes—but with each passing day the round face of the baker's daughter became the last thing I thought of before turning in. After that first time when I had inspected her while she stood in our courtyard, I didn't see her for a week, and she began to fade gradually from my thoughts, like the figure of a minor character slowly retreating to the rear of the stage after reciting their one and only line. But one morning, in the early dawn glow, I went down as usual to put the kettle on for tea, and there you were—the pair of you, lying naked across the kitchen table, wrapped in a single pale pink sheet, laughing uproariously and drinking straight from the bottle of old plum brandy that Laurence had given me on my fifty-sixth birthday, one month earlier.

My blood ran cold. And yet, when I saw you, I immediately understood that anger was not a reaction I had at my disposal: my age, my crumpled morning face, and my long-sleeved nightgown all argued against an outburst, for fear of making me look like the bitter old woman. *Mal-baisée*, you would have said, right? Your favorite expression in French. *The woman who needs a good fuck.* So I held my tongue and retreated very quietly in my felt slippers to my bedroom before you had time to notice my presence. I did feel angry—I was thirsty, and to have to wait for my first cup of black tea was intensely irritating. But it looked as if I was now a prisoner in my own house, and I had no other option than to stay there, humiliated, in my bed, which had already lost its warmth, and listen patiently through the loose floorboards to your chuckling and sighing. After what seemed like an eternity, I peered out through the lace curtain at my window to see you both reeling through the drizzle, trying to walk in step, because you were still wrapped together in your single sheet, making for the barn where you spent the rest of the day nursing your hangovers and listening to Bruce Springsteen, whereas I went back to the kitchen, and counted the teardrops as they fell one by one into the bread dough I was kneading.

I would have done better to save my tears. In the space of only a few weeks, that dreadful vision became my daily lot. Zaza moved in, and you only left the barn to come to the house for food in the middle of the night. When I was out working in my little vegetable garden, I had to lower my eyes not to see your windowpanes blur with steam. Every night like wild animals you would leave traces of your passage in the kitchen—wild boars ravaged our lawn, and you and Zaza left fingerprints in the butter dish, crumbs of *pain d'épices* on the counter, trails of syrup and coffee along the furniture. When I went through the door in the morning, I could practically map out the path of your lovemaking. The remains of your revels came to me like the vestiges of my own youth—I felt as if I'd come too late to the party, as if never again would I be served a full plate, only one where others had helped themselves first. Never again would anyone treat me like a queen—but when had anyone, ever? What was the source of my nostalgia? I was imagining some glorious past, which presupposed a loss of great proportions, but even Günther's courting of me had remained within the tightly-laced limits of what was reasonable—I, Helen, had never been made to lie on a solid wooden table, to be made love to among the ripening fruit and little pots of cream, the way every morning our love-scarred kitchen whispered to me that, only a few hours earlier, you had made love to Zaza.

A nd yet, in spite of myself, as if I couldn't help it, I tidied up after you, I ran the sponge over the polished wood, I washed the sticky plates of your midnight feeds. Just as decades earlier I'd seen to our entire domestic life during that strange month when you were trying to write fiction (only to produce, in the end, a single poem of disturbing pertinence), so I now went on playing my role, a mixture of elder sister and housekeeper, as if I were not upset by your behavior. Once again, I was cruelly at a loss for words to describe my anger. All I could do, in a manner as methodical as it was mechanical, was keep up appearances. If someone had asked me, I would have answered that my efforts stemmed from a desire, above all, to protect Ludwig—to keep him from seeing his father with his old babysitter, from this blurring of boundaries, Oedipus, manhood, and so on—but the truth was that Ludwig was astonishingly impervious to what was going on. He'd just turned sixteen, and was a silent, delicate adolescent, who spent most of his time locked in his room listening to his records. So, I was left to my own resources. And my rage began to grow. But what could I say, in the end? It was your house, not mine. You certainly had the right to bring home and fuck whoever you wanted in your own house. Why should you terminate your love life just because I was living there? We'd never explicitly set any boundaries in all the years we'd lived together. Nor had you committed to spending every night of your life with me. You'd taken me in, on your property, as your best friend, not as your wife. At the outset, I had come to relieve you of your burden, to support you, not to complicate things. As for you, you were honoring your part of the bargain. You went on painting, more and more, and you looked after your son—you would go walking together across the damp meadows, you did not neglect him, you were there for him. You were perfectly free to choose to live shut away in your studio with your new conquest if you so desired. You were not in the wrong. When it was over, perhaps you would come and knock at my door once again, and then I could decide what was the right thing to do. For the time being, I was not on stage. In this act, my character had no lines.

One day as I was driving home at the end of the afternoon, I spotted Zaza in her blue raincoat, walking by the side of the road. She was on the wrong side, her back to the traffic, and in the relentless September rain she was almost invisible—and for a brief moment I thought that one must either be in love with her, or fear her, as I feared her, to instantly recognize her from behind. That first time I simply avoided her, splattering her as I went by. But afterwards, as I continued on my way, trembling like a leaf, muttering *bloody stupid to walk like that in the dark, I could have killed her*, I suddenly heard my own voice. It occurred to me that I could easily have killed her, on that deserted road. At the end of the day, in the Percheron fog. In a gentle yet dense rain, it would not take much to hit her going round a bend, to send her flying into the ditch. And who would be there to see me? Who could testify to what I had done? And even if—even if, through some extreme misfortune, I was seen and denounced—*denounced*, an interesting choice of word, no doubt betraying my feeling of impunity that has subsisted, in spite of everything, to this day—I could always argue that I thought I'd hit a deer. By then I was over fifty-five, and the ophthalmologist in La Ferté-Bernard could attest to my poor eyesight. *For pity's sake, Helen, do me a favor, switch on the light when you read,* he'd pleaded, smiling gallantly, the last time I'd seen him. Everyone knew that the local wildlife, banished from the fields by farming, had a tendency to leave their forest refuge behind for open territory at the first opportunity. If I had indeed collided with an animal, it would surprise no one that I didn't get out of the car to go and have a look—it was the local men who always wanted to go and see, because if the animal was edible they would load it into the boot of the car and thus consider it due compensation for the damage caused to their automobile. But I was a foreigner, a slender woman in her fifties, who couldn't even correctly identify the different varieties of sweet apples, so why would I get out of my car in the dark to inspect a dying fawn I would, in any case, not have had the strength to stuff into the car? I would say I'd been frightened. I would say it was an accident. My eyes filling with tears, I would fold my arms nervously across my chest, and everyone would believe me.

No, coming up with excuses was not the hardest thing. The long years I'd spent analyzing texts had taught me the art of proof. But why did I want to kill Zaza? What did I hope to gain from her death? That you would forget her? That you would come back to me? But you had never left me, after all. If anyone had left, it had been me, without question. Otherwise, you and I had lived together for over half our lives. There might not be any Madame Appledore, but for all that, what other couple had you been in, other than the one you had made with me all these years? And so, I don't even know whether I really wanted to kill her. No. I think I just wanted to be rid of the humiliation of seeing you prefer, even momentarily, such a vacant girl, provocative in the most banal way. Everything about her irritated me—her name, her Ford Fiesta arrogantly parked in our lane, her round face without any sharp definition, her blue-gray eyes, her chubby calves, her lack of manners, her clothes, which I washed. When I stared out the window at her, I instinctively ran my fingers over the hard muscles of my marathon-runner's abdomen, and despised her with every fiber in my body. I would stand in front of the antique mirror in my little bathroom at night, and think of the books I had written, the countries I had seen, the languages I could translate from, I thought of what I had done with my life, the things I'd survived, the men I'd conquered, the knowledge I had acquired, my clear-sighted discernment, the praise I had garnered for my work, all my diplomas in their black and gold frames, everything I had learned because I read books, and everything I knew about you, Frank Appledore, and had never told a soul. In the shiny surface of my looking glass I observed the small, delicate features of my face, and thought of Zaza's graceless build, her lack of style, her big feet and the obtrusive footprints they left in the sand on our drive. It was not so much her actual death I sought, as for justice to be served, I wanted to right the order of the world, according to my understanding of it, to protect that which belonged to me and which all too often I had almost lost—several times before she was even born. I wanted at the very least to sleep through the night without thinking about her. To sleep again. To find consolation for the ripeness of age, and not have to confront the texture of her skin in the morning light, on my terrace.

In the beginning, I was angry at her for being who she was and for being there, to put it simply—but as time went by, to my great astonishment, I began to understand that things were even worse than I had imagined. You were in a constant state of bewilderment, like a young father short on sleep, in a daze—except that it was not your child who got you into this state, but a capricious twenty-eight-year-old lover. I initially thought your lack of orientation was the external sign of your love for her, the ransom of passion, in a way, until I realized that it was not love that exhausted you. You were simply exhausted. It was not Zaza's frisky youth that drove you, it was her perpetual dissatisfaction. You were like the owner of a café who cannot keep up with the demands of his customers, running from one table to the next under a volley of disparate and contradictory orders, watching as dishes grow cold in his hands before he can get them to the right table, and ice cubes melt in glasses before they can quench anyone's thirst, while voices everywhere are constantly shouting out errors in orders. She made you feel needed. For already four months you had not done any serious work. Thirty years earlier, when you had preferred the lovely Anna to me, I had certainly not been as irritated as this—I'd been deeply unhappy, but Anna respected your work, she understood you, she had things to offer you that I did not, she had a gallery, she loved art. In Normandy in 1994, the more time went by, the more appalled I was by

Zaza's stupidity and greed, her inability to tolerate boredom, and the way she had, in so little time, managed to make you believe that she was not merely unbearable and uncultured, no, but gifted rather with some sort of hypersensitivity—a bit like a delicate princess in a fairy tale. That woman. That well-padded girl from Normandy who'd done poorly at school, who lacked all grace. She would weep in your arms. She said terrible things about all the men she'd known before you, and then she went and praised them. She would fail to show up when you'd arranged to meet. She would let you do things that were so bold, physically, that for two whole weeks your aches and pains prevented you from going to the barn to paint, because the weight of your arm at the easel was suddenly greater than you could bear, from utter lack of sleep. She occasionally withheld sex from you, without any explanation, but furiously. She told you—and you later told me—that when she lived in Paris she could not see a single tree from the window of her tiny studio, and that after a moment of heavy silence she had murmured, in conclusion, *My window was sad.* Your French was not all that good, and you thought she'd been speaking literally, poetically attributing emotions to a window frame, and you thought it was sublime. Don't lie, now, Frank. You had tears in your eyes when you told me that story. And I felt like screaming. All she meant was that she lived in a dump. She was a coarse country girl, and selfish. For a reason I'll never know, she'd found you, and was using you. It was as if you yourself had brought her up badly, this girl you'd met when she was twenty-seven. You'd only been seeing each other for a few months, but already she spent entire days not giving a toss about your well-being, whereas you, you watched over her while she slept at night, mindful of her every breath, as if she were a newborn baby. When you tried in spite of everything to have a discussion with her, or raised any serious objection, she would respond with her chiming laugh. Then something became perfectly clear to me. If you stayed with her, you would stop painting, and you would be transformed into the perfect butler—for her. In the best-case scenario. But you *would* stop painting. What I mean is that in doing what I did, it was not solely because I hated her, I also did it to set you free and restore you to your art. Because your art was me. It was thanks to me that you painted. It was thanks to me that you had even found your vocation. Over sixty years ago you set sail upon my bravery as if it were an ocean liner. For years, all those years when you didn't know what to do with yourself, you followed me everywhere, you used my ambitions as a student as an excuse to leave your family, just as you took advantage of my need for tidiness to live in an impeccable house without ever having to clean it. Think about it. Think about it now, finally. If I had not pleaded your case with your father. If I had not taken you with me to Amsterdam. If I had not introduced you to Charlie; if we had not gone together to drink a cup of tea at his place; if we had not been invited to his place because in fact he was hoping to seduce me—where would you be today? And who would you be, Frank Appledore? You would surely rather tell me that I've got it all wrong, that I had nothing to do with your art—but need I remind you that you could not even tear yourself away from my house? When you came to work there, despite the studio you'd set up at Anna's place: what was I to think, other than that you needed me? And when you welcomed me with open arms, when you called me to the rescue from across the ocean, when you entrusted your son to me? You were forever returning to me. It was my position in the world: I was the place you came back to. The way others travel to their birthplace for their health, it seemed to me that you were always irresistibly coming back to be near me, as if I were your home, as if I were your essence, your center. I was the one who protected you, who had always protected you—and above all, I protected you from yourself. You never asked me for a thing, that is true—but Frank, from the very day we met, your incompetence called to me like a siren in the mist.

When a person is as unobtrusive as I am, no one can imagine they might have a passionate temperament. People think my personality is some sort of white noise, that the silence I emit in society is the echo of the silence that has always resounded in the closed space of my mind, beneath my neatly combed hair. But—and I know this better than anyone—you must not judge a book by its cover.

Kill Zaza in a road accident: I found myself toying with the idea more and more often, like a kitten mechanically grabbing at a piece of yarn. With hindsight, I find it hard to admit that I might have been thinking of her death on a daily basis, even as I ran into her on just as daily a basis in our house. There were times when I had sunk so deep into my thoughts that I didn't hear her enter the kitchen without knocking to get a glass of wine or a spoon, and suddenly there she was, the object of my hatred, standing in front of me in the clothes she'd stolen from you, and I heard myself mouthing inane pleasantries with a smile, *Morning, Zaza, everything all right? So you're still in the region, I see?* when what I felt like shouting was, *Still in my house? Why, why, why are you still in my house?* I would have liked to say, *Why are you doing this to me? Is it because I didn't pay you enough, back then, when you were just my child's babysitter? Can I pay you now, so that you will stop coming here?* But it was too humiliating for me. For Zaza, it was simply annoying. When I spoke to her she would murmur something without looking at me, the sort of ready-made replies that young women tend to give women their mother's age to get rid of them, and the moment she was gone I fell headlong back into my fantasies of murder, the way one returns after an interruption to a thousand-piece puzzle. In my bath, at the market, or on my knees in the vegetable garden, no matter when, I immersed myself in my visualization of the accident: acceleration, the thud of the collision, the colors of the ferns in the headlamps. I thought about it every day, all the time, I even went so far as to increase the number of times I went out in the car to up my chances, statistically, of running into her on the road, but the days passed, and my efforts remained futile. I ended up believing it would never happen, that I'd had my chance, and let it slip by. I tried to reason with myself, to convince myself that it was better that way.

And then, one evening, a few weeks before All Saints'
Day, on my way home from a film in Alençon, she
appeared before me again, as if by magic: as I came out
of a bend, there she was, walking with her head down, wearing
her same old raincoat. It was like a private encounter; I
switched off my headlamps, and swung the wheel.

REPERCUSSIONS

She didn't die.

I hit her, but she didn't die.

After I'd spent a sleepless night full of uncertainty, tossing and turning and wondering what the next day would bring, it was Laurence who told me everything. I'd been up since five A.M., distraught, and wandered aimlessly about the house, incapable of tackling the meanest chore—only when either you or Ludwig came into my field of vision did I lower my eyes and pretend to be concentrating on the illegible lines of text in the galleys in front of me on my desk. Weeks later, when I was emptying out my writing desk, I came upon the pencil I'd been holding that morning, and recognized it from the deep gashes my teeth had made in it. Why didn't I say anything to you? Because I didn't know what to say. *I tried to kill your girlfriend last night, Frank, but I don't know whether I succeeded.* It seemed to be totally beyond me to say those words. And so, as soon as it was ten o'clock, which seemed an acceptable time to go and knock at Laurence's door and pretend I was on my way back from the shed that was by the spot where our two properties met, I put on my coat and went out. I wondered how to bring up the subject with her, how to ask my question without giving myself away. But Laurence saved me the trouble, for no sooner had she opened the door than she cried:

"Did you hear, Elsa was hit by a car yesterday!"

"What sort of car?" I asked, biting my lips when I realized how stupid my question was, but Laurence was far too excited to notice.

"I have no idea," she replied with a shrug, as she walked briskly ahead of me down the corridor to the kitchen. "Sit down, I'll make some coffee. She said she didn't see anything, she barely had time to hear the car before it struck her, and then she fell in the ditch, and stayed there all night, with water up to her bottom, until Jacques the postman found her there this morning on his rounds. Do you take sugar, Helen? I can never remember whether you do."

I pushed away the sugar bowl she set down in front of me.

"But why didn't she get out of the ditch before that?"

Even then, as incredible as it might seem, when I think back, I still hated her for her laziness and lack of resourcefulness. *All night long in the ditch, really?*

"She'd twisted her ankle. This morning the doctor had to cut through her shoe to examine her. And the ditch at that spot is quite deep."

We fell silent. Laurence had lowered her gaze, modestly, with a contrite air, but I could see her eyes were shining. As for me, with my librarian's soul, I was trying to analyze and classify the files she had just handed to me. Car. Postman. Ditch. Ankle.

"So she didn't die?" I asked, after thinking for a few minutes.

"No," said Laurence.

She looked at me, and I could see in her eyes that in one instant she had grasped it all, and immediately afterwards, I also saw her erase from memory the intuition that had just seized her, the way one apologizes for a wrong number or for ringing at the wrong door. And I knew that in one respect, at least, I had got things right: no one would accuse me for what I had done. Which also meant that I would have to carry my burden alone.

I was trembling all over by the time I got home. Part of me was relieved I hadn't killed her—in a cowardly way, I felt innocent, because my plan had failed. And I was trying with all my might not to hear what the other part of me was saying. (The part that was saying *I must finish what I have begun;* the part that had obtained my diplomas, my reputation in independent publishing circles, my books.) More than anything, I was overwhelmed with fatigue, I felt ridiculous, and dangerous—which I was, to be sure—and I was just about to calmly sit down in an armchair with a book, to put my hatred behind me once and for all, when I glanced out the window and saw Zaza's Ford Fiesta pulling up in the drive. A gentle late summer rain was falling. You opened the door to the studio and ran to her through the fat drops. She lowered her window and you spoke for a short while, and then in the end you opened her door, and I saw her smile as you knelt on the gravel to gently maneuver one of her legs out of the car, remove her rubber boot, and massage her ankle with the pads of your thumbs, talking to her all the while. Time seemed to stop. The picture was one of almost unbearable eroticism. You eventually took her in your arms to support her as you walked towards the open barn door, which you closed behind you. Motionless in the house, I felt all my anger well up inside me, intact. I had wanted to kill her, and I'd made a martyr of her. Not only were we not rid of her, you loved her more than ever, with your deplorable taste for damsels in distress. And it is all my fault, Frank, all of it, except for what happened next—no, that was not my fault, if a German freelance journalist happened to call just then, and all I had to do was reach out and pick up the receiver.

Y ou never knew that I spoke to that journalist, did you?
That it was me? You only reproached me for having
the magazine in the house, but you never asked me
why I had it in my possession. I thought that perhaps, over
time, you might have guessed—but your stunned face tells me
otherwise. I'm sorry, Frank. Like the barber in the legend of
King Mark of Cornwall, who shares his unspeakable secret
with a hole in the sand, I spoke into that telephone receiver as
if there were no one at the other end. In the fairy tale, rushes
grow where the hole once was, and when the wind blows
through them, they sing of King Mark's shame: his horse ears.
I spoke to the journalist. The very thought that Zaza still
existed, that she was going to continue living with us, continue
coming in and out of my house as she saw fit, continue manip-
ulating you and endangering your work, made me so nervous
that I plunged into an unstoppable flow of words. I literally
dictated the man's article to him. I don't think he knew exactly
what he was after when he called—I think a senior editor had
asked him to call you, and he was simply obeying, without any
real hope of getting any interesting information out of you. But
I wrote his article for him. Since I'd failed so recently to kill
your young mistress, I used a weapon that was more familiar to
me than the alliance between radiator grills and the wet road
from Alençon—I used words. Deploying the same mastery
with which I'd described Andersen's stay with Dickens,
Perkins's influence over Hemingway, Wolfe and Fitzgerald, or

Tolstoy's labor over *War and Peace*, I shared your most terrible secret with that stranger's voice on the line. I told him you abandoned the pregnant Freja without an ounce of remorse. That she died in sad, sordid circumstances. And that was the price you paid to get yourself a son.

In the weeks that followed, I could still have back-tracked. I could have blackmailed the journalist, perhaps, or bought his silence. He left me his number, and I could have called him back to beg him not to print what I'd told him, arguing that we'd never spoken of it with Ludwig and emphasizing his youth, fragility, and innocence. I could at least have stopped the article finding its way into our home. This was before the advent of the Internet, after all, it was an era when information only reached you if you actively went looking for it. It was a German magazine, minor even in Germany—the odds that we'd hear about it in the depths of our Percheron countryside were virtually nil. I could have stood in the journalist's way. And nothing would ever have happened. But I didn't. When he called me back one day, weeks later, to tell me the article would soon be published and he would be only too happy to send me a copy of the magazine, I was arranging slices of fruit on shortcrust pastry, trying to ignore the unbearable squeaking of the rocking chair Zaza was sluggishly moving back and forth three yards away from me, sitting in underpants and a T-shirt, and I heard myself reply in smooth tones, the voice I would have used had a radio reporter rung to tell me I'd won a prize, precisely that voice. And even with that voice there was just one thing to say and I did not say it. When the journalist offered to send me personally a copy of my nastiness, I didn't say, *no, thank you*, or *there's no need*, I didn't say that under no circumstances would that lethal object, forged on a day of great anger, cross the threshold of my house—I said, *yes, with pleasure.* And when the package arrived a few days later, without batting an eyelid I reached for the antique enamel paper knife you'd bought for me at an auction a few months earlier, and removed the magazine from its brown paper wrapping.

Captivated by what I'd told him, the journalist had apparently set about delving further into your sudden fatherhood. He patiently followed the trail back to Freja, and even managed to interview her former colleagues in the ballet company. Anonymously, a handful of dancers evoked Freja's despair at your abandoning her, her financial difficulties during her pregnancy, and the magnificent courage with which she had immediately started practicing again after giving birth—all in order to regain her original athleticism and the strength of her limbs so as to make a living and provide for Ludwig. There was even a thin portfolio of photographs taken in the dressing rooms and on the bus during the tour, and the most poignant showed Freja lying on a blanket in the last row, breastfeeding a tiny Ludwig, with the entire landscape passing in a blur behind them. The article stated that up to three weeks before her death she'd written to you constantly, and that you never replied. If one is to believe what was written there, she didn't even have your address, and on the envelope she simply wrote *Frank Appledore, Amsterdam*—yet still, I cannot believe that you never received any of them, despite your claims to the contrary. Page after page, the face of this young woman I'd never seen, who died over fifteen years ago, whose story I fed to the press, stared up at me with her clear German eyes. I didn't understand what I had done. I couldn't believe it. I didn't believe it. I put the magazine on the third step of the living room stairs, in the spot where Ludwig knew I left the books I liked, and where I also knew that, because he trusted my literary taste, he often came to help himself. You see, it would take the combined action of these multiple little deeds for the catastrophe to occur. My fifty-sixth birthday, a difficult menopause, Zaza's return, *Oh, they must think you're my sister*, and *What can you tell me about Frank Appledore?* and a pink ankle massaged in the rain, and an odd telephone call just at the right moment, and a blue raincoat, and ten pages of pure cruelty. I placed my love for you, my insane love, my passion for you, before our child. Worse still, like Medea slitting the throats of her own sons to punish Jason for daring to repudiate her for a younger woman, I flexed our son's supple body like a bow to shoot the poisoned arrows of my revenge.

And so, one December evening, at dinner, a few weeks after he turned seventeen, Ludwig set the magazine on the table in front of you.

"Ah-hah," you said cheerfully. "What's this?"

You picked up the magazine and leafed through its glossy pages until you came upon the ignominious article. Your eyes grew wide with terror, and not looking at Ludwig you said:

"Where did you get this?"

"I found it in Helen's things. It says Freja was a drug addict and you abandoned her when you found out she was pregnant with me. Is it true, Frank?"

Perhaps only then did you realize what you had done. Eighteen years earlier it had probably cost you no effort to banish Freja, but now you had to answer for what you'd done before her child. Ludwig was looking you straight in the eye, with that pure gaze of his; he was hanging on your every word, full of hope. He was ready to hear everything, ready to accept any version that would erase the one he'd read and reread before he dared come to question you. I think that I, too, in that moment, came to a brutal realization of the consequences of my actions. We never told Ludwig how his mother died. When we had to, we repeated the euphemism his mother's side of the family had used: *a domestic accident.* In the early days when I was taking care of Ludwig, I judged Freja very harshly—*How dared she do drugs,* I would think to myself, indignantly, *when she had such an extraordinary child?* But

Ludwig rarely slept through the night, and a few weeks of sleepless nights later, I poured myself a huge glass of merlot soon after putting him to bed, and I ceased to have an opinion on the matter. *Domestic accident.* I'd nearly forgotten, by force of repetition, that it wasn't true. But there, in the article, the exact words were printed in black and white. *Heroin overdose.* And this was the first Ludwig had heard of it. The article was not only a sordid denunciation of your shortcomings, on which it focused heavily, but also—thanks to the journalist's research—a precious source of information for Ludwig, because it was proof that, somewhere, there were people who *remembered* his mother, who viewed her life as memorable, who'd laughed with her and loved her and stood by her when times were hard. All you remembered was the little boy's distress when you took him in, but you never gave a thought to the life he might have lived with his mother, to the three turbulent years spent among tutus and echoing velvet rooms, or to the intense love that had clearly united them, mother and child, when they were alone in the world and inseparable. Through your obstinate silence, out of fear, too, you made a clean sweep of all that, and you deemed that Ludwig's real life began when he came to live with you, but that wasn't true at all, obviously. The child had memories, and the article was a Pandora's box, enabling him to stick the pieces back together. The dinner table was half cleared, still littered with the plates of cake we'd had for dessert, and we made a strange triangle, you and I transfixed by our respective shame, and our son, his gaze riveted on our lips, begging us to say something, to tell him it wasn't true, that the magazine was a rag and his mother died with dignity. If we'd had time, if things had taken a different course, he would surely have calmed down, would have been able, over time, to curl up with his memories, construct a new self, make a place from which he could enter the entire world still to be discovered—but that time was not granted to us.

Confronted with our damning silence, Ludwig closed his eyes with infinite sadness.

"So it's true. I think deep down I knew it. The article said I was next to her when they found her. I'd forgotten, but now I remember. I waited hours for her to wake up. I was hungry. I'm ashamed when I think about it, but I was hungry, and I kept calling to her, and she didn't move. Afterwards, all I remember is a lot of voices, and then my grandmother Grete's house. After that I came here with you."

"I'm sorry, Ludwig," we heard you murmur.

"Sorry?" asked Ludwig. "But it's all your fault, Frank."

Whereupon Ludwig got to his feet, abruptly.

"You abandoned her. You abandoned us. All for your painting. What are you sorry for? You're never sorry about anything. I know you. You live your life, and you never see anyone but yourself. Helen takes care of everything. You don't know a thing. You think that you're my father because we go for walks in the country, but you only ever talk about yourself all the time. You don't know a thing about me. You never even thought of telling me about my mother. Don't you miss her? I do. But I couldn't find the words to talk about her. It's too hard. That's what I've been thinking about, all these years, whenever I'm with you. I was trying to find the words to make you talk about my mother. Freja. But I was afraid of hurting you, because you told me that she left you. So I thought, she left, and then she died, and he won't ever be able to tell her he loves her. But you never did love her, did you. The questions I never dared to ask you: all the answers are there. You lied to me. About the most important thing. That's what you did. And you can't undo it."

He ran out of the room, like a fawn, and we heard the front door slam in the void. All these years that picture of him has been etched in my brain: the dignity and sadness veiling his delicate face as he bounded out of the room, leaving the two of us, you and me, facing each other over the ruins of dinner.

We looked at each other for a long time, gazes meeting, as if we were lost in what had just happened, trying to process what we'd learned, to understand. So that's it, you were thinking, I, Helen, was the one who was responsible for the magazine showing up in the house. So that's it, I was thinking, you told Ludwig that it was Freja who left you. I understood what you'd done, although I condemned it, but I don't think you managed to find an explanation for why I'd left an article that was so dangerous for you—for *us*— in a place where our son could find it. And I think it was because you failed to resolve the enigma that you eventually opted for anger. Rather than take your son's well-founded reproaches into consideration and go tearing after him, you decided to turn on me.

"Why did you come here?" you asked, after a long silence. "Why, why did you come, Helen, why are you here?"

And that was the beginning of our worst argument. I told you I'd come for both of you, and you said, no, I'd come for myself, because I was sick of my marriage and refused to admit it. I said that it was equally your fault if I'd never been able to be with someone. And yet, you said, you hadn't been with me in Boston when my marriage began to founder, and you had no part in it. I said I couldn't be with someone, knowing that you looked down on them, and that you'd never made any effort to get to know Günther. Then you said, if Günther was so interesting, why would anyone have to make an effort to get to know him. I replied that you knew very well what I meant by that. You said that all you saw was that I was blaming you for not making the kind of effort that I myself should have made. You said that I'd never known what to do with myself, that I was always pestering you, that you too would like to be rid of me, that you'd wanted nothing better than for me to stay in Boston, that you'd never asked me to help you, that in any case you could have looked after Ludwig on your own, how much of a worse job could you have done, anyway? You had entrusted your child to me and now look. I told you you had no right to speak to me like that. You said you were Frank Appledore and you could speak however you bloody liked. I grabbed a hammer from the work bench, raised it above my head, shook it, then put it down.

"There's no point in killing me, Helen," you said, looking me straight in the eye, "when you've already taken what I love most."

We were in the dining room screaming at each other, circling the table like wild animals, setting our most treacherous arguments against each other, our oldest memories, our pettiest grudges, moving each pawn like two grand masters who know one another's game inside out. We had to admit that in forty-four years we'd learned how to argue with each other, the way others have learned how to dance, but this clash, alas, was our magnum opus, our bravura passage, a perfect alignment of the planets so we could tear each other apart in the huge moonlit dining room in that house in the middle of nowhere, as if we'd been waiting all our lives to do just that. But I was exhausted, and the shame I felt was so powerful it made me dizzy. How could I have done such a thing? The more I faulted you for things, the more I could see, as I listed them, a coherence beginning to form, something fated, a trajectory as straight as a bullet's. Our parents. Your failed exams. Your great dependency on me. My excessive need for formality, precision, gratitude. The sudden discovery of your vocation. Anna. Günther. Your paintings like so many attempts to corral me through the post. Ludwig in the arrivals terminal. Normandy. The house in Normandy. Our nights together, again. Your incredible paintings. Zaza in the courtyard.

"It's Zaza," I sobbed, in the end, exhausted. "It's because of Zaza! She—"

"What do you mean, Zaza? What does Zaza have to do with any of this? What the fuck do we care about Zaza right now, for Christ's sake, Helen? I'm talking about my son!"

I could not stop crying now. When you shouted those two last words, *my son*, I realized what I had done. Your son. My son.

For over three hours we screamed at each other before we smelled the smoke. You opened the front door, and we saw the barn in flames.

L udwig set the fire before he fled, so we learned afterwards, and the turpentine took everything with it. It was a vision from hell—the massive wooden structure devoured by flames in the night, in the depths of the country, illuminating everything around it and making our tear-stained cheeks hot. Remember? We stood together in the doorway of the house, watching the disaster unfold, and only a few seconds later did we emerge from our stupor enough to wonder where Ludwig was.

We looked everywhere for him, in the house, the garden, as far as the road, shouting—but he was nowhere to be found. Alerted by the neighbors, the fire brigade came with their hoses to extinguish the fire, and while they were dousing the barn, we begged them to look for our child, but the deep darkness of night and Ludwig's age deterred them, convinced as they were that it was merely a simple teenage sulk, that the boy had gone to seek refuge in his favorite clearing after a volley of parental scolding. They didn't know what sort of family we were. They didn't know that it was Ludwig who set fire to the barn, because we didn't tell them. The friendly, relaxed, young firemen wove us a mantle of reassuring words, but after they left we didn't sleep all night, we paced back and forth along the edge of the forest with our torches, both of us, shouting as loudly as we could, looking for our child, in vain, interrupted in the middle of our quarrel, united in fear for a lack of anything else, holding hands so as not to lose one another in the dark woods.

It was December 22, 1994, and it was the last time I ever held your hand, Frank Appledore. I know I should remember nothing beyond my terror at having lost the trail of my child, I should have forgotten absolutely everything else about that night, but it simply is not so—what I remember is your burning hand and how I clung to it, Frank, and how happy I was, almost, that the distressing discovery of Ludwig's disappearance and the indifference of the firemen and our decision to go looking for him had brought a temporary halt to your reproaches, as if the deeper reasons for the argument had suddenly been invalidated by this miraculous truce. I think of it all the time, the way one remembers the sweetest moments of a night of love.

A man out walking found Ludwig the next morning at dawn, hanging from a branch by his belt, in the forest at the end of the road.

AFTERMATH AND NOW

That was where they led, our endless rambles through Rome, the passionate letters we wrote one another, our thousands of nights spent talking. That was where my devotion led, my patience, the sacrifices I made for our sake. A murder. All that love, in all the wrong proportions, led to a tree. Who knows? Perhaps you'd even painted that tree. Perhaps on our walks we'd even gone right by that tree, never knowing that one day it would mark the definitive end of a part of ourselves.

We were told, in the aftermath of his death, that Ludwig had been psychologically fragile, that the loss of his mother so young and in such traumatic circumstances could not help but leave a lasting effect on him, and that the magazine article would surely have revived painful memories—not to mention the fact that his early childhood, being dragged around here and there, had left him unstable, and that as an adolescent his mother had been diagnosed as bipolar by at least one specialist, an affliction that could be hereditary. We were told all sorts of things, the most intelligent among them by far being that suicide is always inexplicable, intolerable to those who are left behind. But, of course, he didn't kill himself simply because of that argument. He didn't kill himself simply because of that article. I think he killed himself because he'd lost heart: seeing how we were, you and I, was not an incentive for him to grow up and love, or to live a long life. And I feel so sorry for him, and for you, and for myself, I am full of compassion for all three of us. Real parents wouldn't have done that, I thought; real parents wouldn't have wasted time arguing, mindless of where their child had run away to, wouldn't have devoted three hours to their anger when what mattered was their son's sadness. I thought of the judgment of Solomon, in the first book of Kings, when he suggests cutting into two equal halves the infant being fought over by two prostitutes, both of whom claim to be the mother, and he deduces who the real mother is when she chooses to give up her child to her rival rather than see it put to death. What sort of parents indulge in the luxury of a quarrel when their child has gone missing? What sort of parents roar with pride and anger when their unhappy son runs away from them? But we did something even worse than that. In the short weeks that followed Ludwig's death—and I myself don't even know how this happened—we continued to live together. Already the day after the fire Zaza disappeared as if by magic, as if she'd never existed. We probably should have done the same, Frank, but we didn't. We organized the funeral, tidied and folded Ludwig's belongings, informed our families, signed various documents, and went on eating together, breaking bread face to face in the kitchen where we'd seen our child, mad with rage, for the last time. We went on kissing each other good night when we passed one another in our pajamas, by the door to his empty room. Two days after the tragedy, Christmas Eve, we made a fire in the fireplace, and we ate, and drank a glass of the wine I'd bought a week earlier, the very day, if my memory serves me, the German magazine arrived in the post. The following day I weeded the garden, and you spent all afternoon removing the burned wooden planks from your barn before you sat down to draw the plans for the new studio you wanted to build—for a while life still held together like that, and then suddenly it was over. It was I who left, but perhaps it was only because the house belonged to you, and so it seemed logical that I should be the one to leave. You didn't say anything. You didn't need to say anything, in the end. Because even amidst all that overwhelming tension, amidst the catastrophe, we were still inextricably linked, and without a word being said, I believe you knew what would happen, that I would leave at the precise moment when it became necessary for both of us. Just as we had found one another forty years earlier outside the door to the house on Prinsenstraat, punctual down to the last stride, just as we've run into each other today, we left each other in a shared convulsion of horror, in Normandy, in the early days of January, 1995, a little over a year after that wonderful evening when Soto said to me that you and I were made for each other, that it was fate.

That was twenty-three years ago. Even today, when I think of Ludwig's death—which I do all the time, Frank, all the time—I still cannot believe that less than a mile away from where I stood—I, his adoptive mother who'd sworn to protect him, who'd entered his life desiring nothing more than to be a refuge for him—my seventeen-year-old son, alone in the icy forest in the last days of the year, decided to make a solid knot in his leather belt and put an end to his life. So near. I still cannot get used to the idea that he is no longer alive on this earth, that he has disappeared forever. That his body and voice no longer exist. That all this time the tiny creatures of the earth have been devouring my child, and that this is in the order of things. In my dreams, of course, he never dies. He has grown up. Through some miracle he's reached adulthood safe and sound, he's cut his brown hair, and it is strange to see him at that age, but he is alive. Our son—because I can refer to him like that, after all, now, for the first time, without being afraid someone might correct me—our son would be forty years old this year, if he hadn't killed himself. Can you picture him? The final verses of "Funeral Blues," that famous poem by Auden, often chime deep in my memory, mysteriously:

> *I thought that love would last for ever: I was wrong.*
> *The stars are not wanted now: put out every one;*
> *Pack up the moon and dismantle the sun;*

Pour away the ocean and sweep up the wood.
For nothing now can ever come to any good.

Sweep up the wood, Frank. Remember. In Rome, where we went, we almost always had to go around the Forum and the Colosseum to get anywhere, the way events in life, past and present, spring to mind with every movement we prepare to make, and we have to learn to make our way around them. If I have forgiven myself—and I suppose I must have, since I'm still standing here, breathing in London's cool April air, since I didn't kill myself as a result of my child's death; it must mean I have forgiven myself, at least in part—inevitably, I must have forgiven you, too.

I think that even during the fire it struck me as strange that you were not mourning the fate of your paintings. Later, in the days that followed, this gave me a certain comfort, to know that at least you weren't thinking about them at the time—but you eventually and unwittingly proved me wrong, when in the course of a conversation you innocently informed me that the day before the tragedy you had sent all your recent work to your dealer, and consequently you immediately knew that you had nothing to fear where your paintings were concerned. And that little detail—that, too, hurt me, more than I would have imagined. In fact, in the years that followed you entered a productive phase that was altogether astonishing. At a time when everyone expected your level to decline, the opposite happened. I went away, but you stayed in the house, you built the new studio according to plan, and you went back to work with a frenzy. And to be honest, I thought you were still there. I think that in the past people desired your paintings because you seemed indestructible, and that now they wanted them because you'd been defeated in the worst way, because your son had killed himself. Killed himself to get away from you, or to punish you. Killed himself in that wonderful forest which his father had painted for years in the most minute detail. It was like the ultimate way of saying he would have liked to occupy another place between us, to be at the center of the painting, and never leave it, to be more important than painting itself. It was at that point that you began sawing your paintings in pieces. But you did go on painting, after Ludwig's death. You didn't disintegrate to the point where you could no longer paint. In fact, it was other people who had to remind you, I think. Later on, in museums, I even came upon that infinitely personal detail carefully printed on the little notices next to your paintings: *Frank Appledore, oil on canvas. The artist completed this work after his only son hanged himself.* I tore the notices from the wall, crying, but the alarm didn't go off, and I never knew why.

What have we done, Frank? I never knew how to explain our adolescence to anyone—our affinity, our constant need for each other over the decades, our disappointment in other people. I know so many words, yet I don't have the vocabulary to explain it to you, Frank Appledore. I have spent my life writing; I do not know how to speak. Only now can I say to you: I loved you, Frank. I wish someone could see us now, the way we are in this moment, facing each other across a street full of noise, in a city where we've never lived together, I wish someone were here to hand down the final judgment. The sun is setting on Primrose Hill. I think I have been quietly talking to you like this for nearly six hours. That was our life, Frank. We will not get another one. That's it. Kiss me. For everything else, it is too late.

Born in Nantes in 1987, Julia Kerninon has a doctorate in American Literature. Her first novel, *Buvard*, has won many awards, including the Prix Françoise Sagan. She was granted a Lagardère young writer's scholarship in 2014. Her second novel, *Le dernier amour d'Attila Kiss*, won the Prix de la Closerie des Lilas in 2016.